LUCY the GIANT

LUCY the GIANT

by Sherri L. Smith

DELACORTE PRESS

Published by
Delacorte Press
an imprint of
Random House Children's Books
a division of Random House, Inc.
1540 Broadway
New York, New York 10036

Visit us on the Web! www.randomhouse.com/teens
Educators and librarians, for a variety of teaching tools, visit us at www.randomhouse.com/teachers

Library of Congress Cataloging-in-Publication Data

Smith, Sherri L.
Lucy the giant / Sherri L. Smith.
p. cm.
Summary: Fifteen-year-old Lucy, the largest girl in her school, leaves her small Alaska town and her alcoholic father and discovers hardship—and friendship—posing as an adult aboard a commercial fishing boat.
ISBN 0-385-72940-5 (trade)—ISBN 0-385-90031-7 (lib. bdg.)
[1. Runaways—Fiction. 2. Family problems—Fiction. 3. Fishing boats—Fiction. 4. Coming of age—Fiction. 5. Alaska—Fiction.] I. Title.
PZ7.S65932 Lu 2002
[Fic]—dc21

2001028173

The text of this book is set in 14-point Filosofia.

Book design by Susan Livingston

Manufactured in the United States of America

February 2002
10 9 8 7 6 5 4 3 2

BVG

To my family, for their support,
and to Nancy, who gave Lucy a name

PROLOGUE

February 28

TEN FEET BELOW THE BERING SEA, ALASKA

They say your entire life flashes before your eyes when you are drowning. So far I've only seen the past few weeks. It hardly seems fair. But I guess when you're fifteen, there's only so much worth remembering. When you're fifteen and you're me.

I see Harley, the way he looked the first night in that bar, and the steam coming out of Tracer's ears when I beat him at shots. I see Santa Barbara rooting around in the trash. And my father, purple with drink and rage, raising his fist. Just images, flashes, not a story like I thought there would be. Nothing that makes any sense. Even now, when I'm drowning, I don't understand most of my life.

I surrender to the water. It's beautiful down here, cold, deep, and softly quiet. Pale green plankton glowing like tiny neon lights. A girl could get used to this. If she didn't have to breathe.

So I do breathe, and the heavy rush of ice water floods my mouth, my lungs. It hurts. My chest aches like it's going to burst. In this flash of pain I see the face, the one I'd forgotten. The one I never thought I'd see again. My mother's.

It is possible to cry underwater while drowning. Because I do.

I haven't seen my mother since I was seven.

Everything that has happened to me since then is her fault.

CHAPTER 1

January 15

SITKA, ALASKA

"You don't belong here."

The door to the bar bangs shut behind me. A burst of cold air and snow follows me inside. It's good to be inside again, even if it is for the wrong reasons. I stand in the doorway until my eyes adjust to the low light.

"Murph, get that kid out of here." The jukebox is blasting, but I can still hear the jeers.

"Everybody knows Lucy's underage," someone calls out.

"Can't tell it for looking, though," someone else laughs. From the doorway, I can't tell who it is. But everyone in Sitka knows me. I'm Joe Otsego's girl, Lucy the Giant.

I scan the tables. My dad isn't in here.

Ignoring their catcalls, I push up to the bar.

"Hey, Murph." I nod to the bartender. He's in the middle of drawing a draft. I look around again and catch my reflection in the mirror behind the bar. Between the bottles my face looks more gray than its usual brown. You look tired, Lucy girl, I tell myself. One day you should just leave him here to rot.

Murph looks up from the tap, neon lights shining off his bald head. "He's in back."

"Thanks." I squeeze past the barstools, work boots, and peanut shells to the stockroom, the "back." Rows of metal shelves filled with boxes of liquor, beer kegs, you name it. Enough booze to fuel the town for the next century. Or at least to make it through the week.

He's where he always is, passed out facedown on the cement floor, his secondhand army jacket thrown over him like a blanket. Usually Murph only calls me when Dad has one of his rages on, when the booze that usually just makes him slow and stupid hits a trigger somewhere and he goes up like a bonfire. All you can do then is stay out of his way and clean up the mess when it's over. And call me to bring him home. As for me, I know enough not to show up until then.

I shove his arms into the jacket sleeves and drag him up into a fireman's hold. "Come on, you've got to help me a little bit," I grunt, tossing his arm around my shoulders, lifting up under his armpits. This way it'll look like we're staggering out together. Not like I'm carrying him, which I am.

He never even opens his eyes. The toes of his boots drag, leaving little trails in the sawdust on the barroom floor. No one says a word on our way out.

"Thanks, Murph," I mumble, and head out the door.

I can't see the truck, so I don't know if he parked it here or hitched a ride with one of his buddies. It doesn't matter. I just started driver's ed in the fall and don't quite trust myself behind the wheel. Especially now that it's starting to rain. The early-January snow will melt and turn to ice before long.

Bending down, I drop one of his arms and grab his leg. Another grunt and he's slung across my back like a deer.

"Home again, home again," I puff. Jiggedy-jig.

Lucky for me my dad's a small man, or I'd never get him home at all.

I kick the door open with my toes. We never keep it locked. There's nothing to steal, and nobody who'd try anyway.

I stumble through the mudroom and the kitchen and dump my dad on the living room sofa. He groans, rolls over, and goes back to sleep.

"All right then. You're welcome." I go back to the

mudroom, take off my boots and coat, and go upstairs to my room.

—/—

It's five o'clock in the morning and the house is silent. I think if I can just lie here and be quiet it will stay this way, perfect, forever. Instead, I shift to get comfortable. My hand thwacks against the wall. I bump my head on the angled ceiling and curse under my breath, knocking into a few more things before I'm safely up.

I stopped marking the inches on my doorjamb when I passed six feet. I haven't grown much since then, but enough to make getting out of bed almost impossible. My room is so small I can't even really stretch my legs in it.

I grab my backpack, a change of clothes, and a coat and slip down from the attic into the kitchen.

I could have a bigger room if I wanted—one that fits me, more or less. But that would mean being closer to wherever my dad is. And that could make any room seem small. It doesn't help to be my size when someone wants to ignore you. So I try to stay low and stay out of his way. Even if that means sticking to my attic with its doll-sized bed and peaked window, and pretending that one day I'll have a place of my own, just right for me.

In the mudroom I swap my pj's for my street clothes, pack a towel, grab my boots, and head out the door. The Laundromat will be open in an hour. It's one of the few left in Sitka with a public shower. With all the seasonal workers and college kids "roughing it" around here, someone decided years ago it was a good idea to have at least one on the way into town from the ferry docks. Since Laundromats have hot running water, they were the natural choice. I come here because public showers are bigger than the one we have at home. I don't bang my head on the faucet or my elbows on the walls. And I don't run the risk of waking up my dad.

Sitka's just waking up. I head down the slope from our house in search of breakfast. Like most towns in southeastern Alaska, Sitka is built like a cat on a bathtub ledge, with its back squeezed up against the mountains like it's afraid of getting its feet wet. It's the kind of town where everyone knows your family and your business, even if they don't always know you by name. Unless, of course, you stand out in a crowd. Like me.

I live up the mountain a ways. Not so far that you need a truck to make it, but out the road enough to keep us from mixing with the summer tourists. Across the blue water of the Sound, Mount Edgecumbe stares back at me—a soft dome capped with snow, but with an oddness about it, like Mount Fuji in Japan, that instantly marks it as a volcano instead of one of the countless mountains around here. It's something to see on a clear day, with the sailboats and the light bouncing off the water. It can make you catch your breath. Now, with the sun still behind the mountains, Mount Edgecumbe practically glows, its snowy head bowed to the water.

I like it early like this, with the stars still hanging overhead. From the look of it, today's going to be one of those rare days without rain. In the summer it would be broad daylight by now, but winter makes most of the day look like twilight. Night birds are still singing in the trees. I tromp down the main road to the McDonald's, the closest thing we have to a twenty-four-hour restaurant here. Something scuffles in the bushes. I pause and see a stray dog skittering through the scrub.

I'm halfway down the hill when I hear deep, mournful noises coming from the Sound. Although I can't see them, I can hear the pod of humpback whales sounding their way through the water. I close my eyes and try to imagine them. Whales. Great big hulking bodies floating like nothing in that icy, calm water. The Sound is full of them this time of year, feeding before they head out to sea.

My mother was a Haida Indian. I have her brown

skin, her black hair, and a story she used to tell me about the days when animals could take on human form. Whales could be people. They could look and talk just like human men and women if they wanted to. Only their size or their love of water gave them away. And whenever they got tired of their human bodies, they could take them off like coats and be whales again. Some days I wish the stories were true. It would explain my size. And why my mother ran off without me.

The song of the passing pod fades, and the sun starts to make more of an appearance in the sky. By the numbness in my fingertips I can tell I've been standing here a long time. That makes up my mind—shower first, and then a nice hot breakfast.

My hair is freezing at the ends, still wet from the shower, when I leave the Laundromat. I cross the road to McDonald's and stop in my tracks. My dad is sitting at a booth in the window with one of his buddies, a straggly scarecrow of a guy named Sam. Water drips down my neck from beneath my hat into my collar. I can't just stay outside and freeze. So I go in.

"Joe, man, ain't that your kid?"

My dad grunts but doesn't budge when I walk through the door. I can see him watching my reflection in the window. I shuffle up the line and order my coffee and hotcakes to go. I had hoped he'd still be home on the sofa. I should've checked before I left. But I didn't.

"Joe, man, it *is* Luce. Hey, Lucy!" Sam yells across the restaurant. "How 'bout joinin' me and your old man?" He waves me over, greasy flannel shirt flapping on his skinny arm like a weathered flag. I close my eyes, wishing the blush I feel growing on my face would go away. You'd think I'd be used to this by now. You'd think everybody in here would be. The other customers cough, or fall silent, or look the other way. I pretend not to hear Sam and hope he doesn't call me again.

The cashier today is Vickie Drake, my old babysitter from ages ago, before my mom left town.

"Hey, Lucy." She gives me my order with a tight little smile and tucks a stray hair into her brown cap. Vickie's feeling sorry for me, I know. I didn't have to be here to imagine the scene a few minutes ago when my dad, half-sick from beer and cold, staggered in here with Sam and harassed her before ordering a sausage biscuit. It happens at least twice a week.

"Thanks, Vickie." I stand up as tall as I can so I don't look quite so helpless to her. This is fine, I tell myself. This is the way a morning should be, father and daughter sharing a meal. I go over to eat breakfast with my dad.

"Hey, little big gal," Sam says. "Doncha got

nothin' to say to your uncle Sam?" He chuckles. "Uncle Sam. I like the sound of that."

But I don't have anything to say to him. Sam could be Chuck or Dave or any of my dad's other wasted friends. Misery loves company, and my dad's got a whole lot of both.

Instead, I spread the butter on my pancakes so thick it looks like icing. As it starts to melt, I drown my plate in syrup.

Sam's still chuckling to himself because he's already a little drunk today. My dad blearily finishes the last of his sausage and coffee.

"Goin' to school today?" He says each word carefully, trying not to slur them together.

"Yessir," I reply.

He nods, wipes his mouth on the sleeve of his used army jacket, and stands up. Patting his pockets for his keys, my dad staggers out with Sam's arm around him. I watch them haul themselves into my dad's pickup truck and wonder how many new dings and scratches it'll have before they make it home.

When I finally look away, my eyes are damp and my hotcakes have gotten cold. To say my dad and I don't talk is an understatement. Say he doesn't even know I exist and maybe you're halfway there. Still, when he does say something, for some stupid reason, it matters.

I wipe my eyes and get a refill on my coffee. Soon enough it'll be time to go to school.

My high school is a stone's throw from McDonald's. By the time I get over there, kids are already cramming into the main hallway. I hang back a ways, letting most of them head in. I tend to tower over all but the tallest boys. Sometimes I take off my hat to try and split the difference, but it doesn't really help. A couple of girls bump into me going up the stairs. They giggle and I recognize them—Tina Martin and Charlotte Baker. We all played together in fifth grade, before I started to really grow. Now I'm not much fun to share clothes with, I guess, so they leave me alone.

"Hello? Who built the wall here?" Charlotte holds up her hands. "Oh, sorry. Just the Giant. Again." They both laugh and weave around me.

"Luce, wait up!" a voice squeaks. When I say squeak, I'm not exaggerating. Sheila Devine's the closest thing I have to a friend, so I wouldn't talk bad about her, but her voice is just as small as the rest of her. Ever since I helped her get out of a locker some senior stuffed her into last year, she's been not so ashamed to talk to me. I've even gotten used to the fact that we look like David and Goliath together.

"Hey, Sheila." I wave and slow down to Sheila-pace, which is like a half step for every two of hers.

Sheila is a hummingbird—all twitter and chitter. She never stops. Her jeans are practically a size zero, and she wears chunky platform sneakers so she doesn't have to climb into her locker to reach the top shelf. That's how that senior nailed her last time. Sheila once told me she has to wear her hair short, because longer than shoulder length it's too heavy for her neck. Compared to Sheila, I'm an ox.

She catches up to me in time to see Charlotte and Tina still giving me looks. Sheila makes a face. "Charlotte Baker is such a toad." She grabs my arm and steers me away from Charlotte, toward our lockers. "Hey, did you get your history test yesterday?"

"Yeah, A minus. What about you?"

"B minus. Maybe we could study together next time. You're like a genius at tests. I could really use an all-nighter."

For a minute, I imagine having Sheila over for a cram session. But an all-nighter at my house usually brings down the cops.

"I can't." I beg off with a shrug.

"No. You *won't.*" Sheila makes a face. "C'mon, Lucy. You could come to my house, you know?"

I could. But then who would Murph call when my dad needs to be taken home? I shrug again. "Maybe another time."

"Okay, okay." Sheila lets it go with a sigh. "I'm

never going to get into Pepperdine with my GPA. I need at least a three point five."

"Relax. They'd be crazy not to take you. And if they don't, so what? Move to California anyway."

"Yeah, right," she snorts. "Like my parents would just pay for me to hang out on the beach and learn to surf."

"You could get a job." I shrug, taking off my backpack. We've got just a few minutes to unload at our lockers before the bell rings.

"Lucy, I'm a kid. I can't get a job worth jack without a degree. I'd be living back at home faster than you could say lickety-split." She sighs again. "Hey, can I borrow your French book?"

It takes a few minutes of digging to find it—my backpack is bigger than the lockers we get here. "I need it back by fourth period."

"No problem. I'll give it to you after gym."

"Don't remind me," I groan. Gym was bad enough when we had basketball and everyone thought I'd be some kind of star. Now we have swimming, which means swimsuits for everyone else, granny suits for me. I hate it.

"Hey, at least you'll get into college." She pulls a long face. "I'm going to be stuck in Sitka working the counter of the Halibut Hut until I'm ninety."

"If you're lucky," I say with a grin. Sheila would look cute in one of those little fish hats, slinging fried fish patties around on buns all day until she melted from the heat and grease. She knows it, too. That's what makes it so scary. The bell rings and we head off to English class. I like Sheila. I almost wish I could invite her over after school. But even if she seems to overlook my size, overlooking my dad passed out on the couch is a different story.

"*The Old Man and the Sea*, people. By Ernest Hemingway. Arguably the greatest work of one of the most important writers of our time." Mrs. Krupke, our tenth-grade English teacher, hauls a cardboard box full of musty paperbacks around the room. As she passes, we each take the best copy we can find in thirty seconds. I always wonder why these books get so chewed up. A kid's backpack is a dangerous place, but even so—missing covers?

Fortunately the cover of my copy isn't missing, so I can see the hot sun beating down on a sheet of dark water. The book is light, too, only a couple hundred pages. Not a problem, with my kind of free time.

"The epic battle between man and fish," Mrs. Krupke continues. "Something I'm sure more than a few of you are familiar with. But this takes place off the coast of Cuba, not Alaska. Consider it a little bit of sunshine this winter and my gift to you. There will be a paper, so no skimming and no renting the movie."

Groans echo across the classroom. Before anyone can ask a question, the bell rings and everyone stampedes for the door. Sheila slips past me and through the crush. I raise my arms over the other kids' heads so I don't elbow anyone in the face, and wade out into the hallway to get my swimsuit for gym.

When school lets out I go to a spot down by the harbor to watch the boats bobbing in the channel. Someday I'd like to get on one of those boats and just sail on out of here. There is a certain attraction to leaving, of course. Like living in a place where I can have friends come over and do homework without my dad stumbling in and making a scene. Or being able to walk into a grocery store without the guy behind the liquor counter calling me Joe's girl. Or not having the McDonald's cashier smiling at me in pity. If the rest of it stopped, I could live with being called the Giant.

But those are only daydreams. I doubt there's anywhere on earth I'd really fit in, except for here in Sitka, cleaning up after my dad. Sheila will probably make it to California one way or another, despite what she says. I, on the other hand, may as well fill out my Halibut Hut application right now.

My watch beeps. The digital face says it's four o'clock. There's laundry to do and old beer bottles to throw away, so I turn my back to the Sound and head home.

Our house doesn't have a view. At least, not one most people would want to look at. My dad's got what's left of a little motorboat he either salvaged or totaled once, half-covered by a plastic tarp stapled to a frame. He calls the boat his project and swears every year it'll be out on the water by June. It never is.

Something brushes up against the tarp, startling me. Probably just a raccoon. But when I turn around, I see that same stray dog from this morning.

"Get out of here, hound. My dad doesn't like dogs." When he's home and sober enough to see straight, he'll take out his old BB gun and shoot at strays from the kitchen window. He's never hit one that I've seen, but I try to hide the BB pellets so he'll never get the chance. Still, if I was a dog, I wouldn't risk hanging around.

The dog gives me a pathetic look. She's knocked over the garbage can and made a mess of the driveway. Lucky for me I haven't thrown out the bottles yet.

"Go on, scoot." I shoo the dog away and set the can upright again before heading for the house.

In the afternoon light our house looks like the loser in a schoolyard fight. The paint's all scratched and peeling from too much rain and ice. One window is blacked out with electrical tape and plywood—another project my dad never completed. Pretty much all of my dad's projects stopped when he realized my mother wasn't coming back. But it's just as well. The plywood hides his passed-out shape on the sofa better than curtains ever could.

Years ago somebody carpeted the three steps to the mudroom with Astro Turf. I scuff some of it up with the toe of my boot stumbling up the stairs.

Inside, the house smells of stale beer and cigarettes. I drop my bag in the mudroom and do my rounds, knocking ashes onto the floor for easier vacuuming and opening the windows that still work to air the place out. The wind picks up and I have to keep my coat on to stay warm, but I'll take the cold over the smell any day. There's sweeping to do, and dishes, once I've picked up all the bottles. We can't even recycle in Alaska. We'd have to ship everything out to Seattle for that.

Five o'clock rolls around and when my dad doesn't come home I figure he must've headed out with his boys early. Usually he's dropped in by now to pick up some money from the kitchen table. I stay in my room until he's gone. In general, I try to leave the house before my dad wakes up, stay away until he's gone out, and be asleep with the radio on by the time he comes home in the morning so I can't hear him retching in the bathroom. On a good day I don't see him at all.

I'm exhausted. Since I've got the place to myself, I collapse right down onto the sagging sofa. My knees are higher than my elbows when I sit here, and it reeks of my dad, but I don't care. It's nice to not have to hide out in my tiny dollhouse of a bedroom.

I'm just starting to doze off when I hear my dad's truck come rattling into the driveway. I bolt like a rabbit for the stairs, but not before he makes it through the front door.

He stands there staring at me, a different drinking buddy—Frank, from the bar—hanging back behind him. I stop running and slowly climb the stairs. After a second I can hear my dad clomp into the kitchen, work boots heavy on the linoleum.

Change scrapes across the kitchen table. "This oughta shut Murph up about the tab," he says. Frank grunts in agreement. A toilet flush and the snap of two beer cans opening, and then they're gone for the night.

Tonight I won't go out looking for my dad. He can sleep on the stockroom floor all winter if he wants to. I root around in my backpack for *The Old Man and the Sea* and start to read.

CHAPTER 2

January 17

SITKA, ALASKA

When I go downstairs this morning, I almost jump out of my skin. My dad is sitting in the kitchen, work boots up on the table, sipping coffee out of a cracked mug like it's the most normal thing in the world. He smiles at me.

"Morning, honey."

I haven't seen that smile in a long time. It makes me drop my bag and stare. I wiggle my toes inside my socks. I can still feel them. I must be awake. "Hey, Dad."

"Going to school today?" He's sober. Saints alive, he's sober. I don't know what to do.

"Yessir."

"How about some breakfast first with your old man?"

It feels like there's a moth between my ears, my

heart's beating so loud in my head. "I'll get my boots on."

"Naw, naw. We'll cook right here. Like we used to. Sit awhile." He waves at an empty chair next to him. I warily drag my bag with me to the seat.

"That's more like it. Want some coffee?"

"Yessir."

He pours me a cup and slides it over. I don't like it black, it's too bitter. But the sugar's not out, so I don't ask.

"So, Luce, how you been? Gettin' to be a big girl now, aren't ya?"

"I suppose," I mumble, and brace myself for the other shoe to drop.

"That's all right then, all right," my dad says to himself. I'm staring at my hands on the tabletop, at the speckled patterns in the linoleum, but I have to look up again. Is he really sober?

He catches me looking. His eyes are dark brown like mine, and clear as day. My heart skips a beat. The sun hasn't come out like this in months.

"Daddy?" I whisper, afraid to break the spell.

"Yeah, baby?"

Baby. He hasn't called me that since I outgrew him. It makes me smile.

"I'll make breakfast."

I rummage through the cabinets to find the only

thing I'm good at besides Pop-Tarts and cereal. Good old-fashioned instant oatmeal. It doesn't go bad for decades and all you need to do is add hot water. I mix up a couple of bowls at the counter and pop them in the microwave. It takes me a minute, but I dig out an old box of raisins from the pantry. By the time I find the maple syrup, things are looking pretty good. The raisins, on the other hand, are so hard they've practically crystallized.

"Got to go shopping soon," I say over my shoulder.

My dad snorts. I don't like the sound.

"Don't know when to keep quiet," he mutters. "Just like your mother." He tosses back his coffee like it's a shot of whiskey. "What's here isn't good enough." He slams his feet on the floor with a bang that makes me jump. "I'm going to work."

"Work?" Stupid. Stay low, Lucy, and out of his way. But my dad hasn't worked in months.

"Girl, you think school makes you smart? Better than me? I work when I want to, and when I don't, it's none of your business. I keep you fed."

He points a finger at me and I realize I'm still holding the spoon, dripping oatmeal onto the floor. My dad shakes his head and storms out the front door.

Way to go, Lucy. Dad's sober about as often as the moon is blue. And it ends in a fight every time. Next time I'll just have the coffee.

Now I'm not hungry anymore. I scoop the oatmeal off the floor and back into my dad's bowl. It's still hot and I don't want to melt a hole in the garbage bag, so I shove on my boots and carry both bowls outside.

There's a dog out by the garbage can. That same stray I saw earlier this week.

"Shoo."

She doesn't budge.

"Get out of here," I snap, and take the lid off the trash.

I don't know if it's the look in her eyes, or the fact that even oatmeal looks pretty good to a dog when it's this cold out. I put my dad's bowl on the ground and shove it toward the dog.

"Careful. It's hot."

She looks at me doubtfully, sniffs the bowl, then lies down in front of it and waits. I sit in the driveway and join her, picking the raisins out of my own bowl before settling in for breakfast. As soon as the dog's oatmeal is cool enough, she tucks in right alongside me.

The oatmeal sticks in my gut like a little heater when it's time to swim laps in gym class. It almost makes the cold water bearable, but it can't do anything about the thin layer of oil that seems to form on the pool by fourth period. I try not to think about it and hurry through my laps. The school's pool isn't a big one. We have to take turns, with most of the kids hugging themselves on the side of the pool or trying to look cool on the benches until it's their turn. I like to get my laps over first. Less time in a swimsuit, more time wrapped in a towel.

My last lap of breaststroke puts me at the far end of the pool, away from my towel. Great. I get out and try to speedwalk to the other end.

"What size bra do you think she wears?" Donnie Simpson nudges one of his friends. He acts like I can't hear him. But I've heard him every day this month, whenever I have to pass by on the way to the shallow end. Although some days it's my underwear or shoe size he asks about instead. I've known Donnie since second grade. I even had a crush on him when we were eight. But then I got tall and he got stupid.

I stop in front of him, unfold my arms, and look down my nose. "Funny how my ears are way up here and I can still hear you."

Donnie shuts his mouth. His friends laugh. "Busted!" I try to hide my smile until I'm wrapped in my towel in the corner of the gym.

"Hey, Lucy." Sheila waves from the water as she dog-paddles her way down the lane toward me.

Sheila's good at a lot of things, but a swimmer she is not. She climbs out gasping and sits next to me on the bench.

"Guess what my brother did last night?"

"Slept?"

"Ha ha. No. He signed on for a tour up north in Kodiak. Can you believe it? And you thought winter was a drag down *here*!"

Sheila's brother Dan is a twenty-three-year-old hotshot who joined the Coast Guard last year and moved to the capital, Juneau, a day's ferry ride from here. I haven't seen Dan in ages, but I've always thought he was kind of cool. Sheila, on the other hand, hates him. "He thinks he's *soooo* important just because he saved a couple of people from drowning," she always complains. It's true. He was a lifeguard in high school and became a local hero for saving some kids at the Y. But Dan's never bragged about it much. He acted like he was just doing his job. I would give my right arm to have a brother like that. But that's me.

"You must be thrilled," I tell her. "Dan sailing around on the Bering Sea freezing his butt off."

"Yeah, until he saves somebody *else's* life and I have to hear 'your brother, the hero' all over again at home."

I laugh. "Well, maybe he'll marry some crab boat

captain's daughter. Then you'll never have to see him again."

"Ladies, this isn't a chat room." The gym teacher, Mrs. Jordan, frowns at us from across the pool.

"Whatever," Sheila whispers to me, and tucks her hair back into her cap. She hops back into the water and does a floundering backstroke, sticking her tongue out at me as she goes.

"Ugh. I hate my life!" Sheila moans as we head toward our lockers. The halls are jammed with winter coats and cold air. It's been raining pretty steadily all afternoon. Everybody wants to get home before the storm really picks up. I push a path through the kids. Sheila follows, complaining.

"Jordan's making me take double-period gym because I didn't do all my laps today."

I pat Sheila on the back. "That's not right. Give her a doctor's note or something. 'Sheila's too delicate to swim.' "

Sheila gives me a playful shove. "Hey! I could take *you* in a fair fight. If I had a tank."

"Oh, thanks." I roll my eyes. " 'Sheila's too *dangerous* to swim.' "

"Please. And what's up with Krupke and that dumb 'Old Man and the Hoohah' book? A twelve-page paper on 'My Biggest Fish'? What kind of crappy topic is that for a paper? And we practically have to write a *novel* to boot."

"Boy, your life *does* suck." I smile.

"Funny funny, ha ha," Sheila replies. "I don't know about *you,* but between choir practice, yearbook, and now swimming, I'll barely have time to finish *reading* the book, let alone write about it."

We reach our lockers and Sheila goes through the ritual of hauling out all her extracurricular crap—gym bag, sheet music, photo proofs.

Sheila is a firm believer in all school and after-school activities. She says it helps beef up your college applications. From what I've heard, she's right, but most kids wait until their senior year before they cram it all in. Especially joining the yearbook committee. Sheila's been doing it all since day one.

"Oh, that reminds me." She hoists the photos into her bag. "School pictures are tomorrow. Know what you're going to wear?"

I haven't had my picture taken since sixth grade, when the photographer started making me stand behind the rest of the class next to a kid perched on a box. *Photogenic* is not the word to describe a giant.

She sees my blank face and sighs. "Lucy, this is important. It's a fall-themed backdrop this year, all right? So you should wear a sweater. Something with a pattern in case they do black-and-white, and dark because it's slimming."

"Don't you mean *shortening*?"

"Ha ha." Sheila smirks. "Don't worry. The camera only gets you from the waist up." She sighs, bent over by the weight of her bag. "Gotta go. You're just lucky you don't have someone waiting for *you* to show up somewhere at three-oh-five every day."

"I guess so," I agree.

But today someone *is* waiting for me. That stray dog, right outside the schoolyard. Get real, Lucy, I remind myself. You can't have a dog.

"Scoot," I tell her. She hunkers down and darts away.

I watch her disappear down the block, then head home to find something dark and patterned.

My dad's gone when I get home. I head up to my room and rummage through a chest of old clothes, trying to find the right sweater to go with my one pair of gray dress slacks. Finally I pull out a dark blue wool sweater positively covered in little fuzzballs. That's kind of like a pattern, I guess.

I spend the next twenty minutes picking off the fuzz with strips of masking tape and wondering if the slacks I've picked out make me look too much like a teacher instead of a kid. I guess it doesn't matter. If I'm going to do this, I'm doing it all the way. Last thing, I pull out a pair of fake pearl earrings with a matching gold-and-pearl necklace I got at the drugstore for my middle-school graduation. I was too chicken to wear them then, but this year will be different.

I put my hair up in a bun. It feels funny off my face, but that way the earrings show. I even toy with the idea of lipstick, but the jewelry feels like enough for one day. I don't look so bad, from what I can see in the mirror, but my mirror's so tiny I can only look at myself a foot at a time. I head downstairs, where the bathroom mirror's bigger. Too late, I hear the truck pull into the driveway. Before I can stop and turn around, my dad is walking through the door.

"Christ Almighty!" he roars. I freeze on the last step. "For a minute there I thought it was Christmas. Them earrings on you look like ornaments on a tree." He jabs at the necklace. "Where'd you get all that anyway?"

My face is tight. I can't even frown. I pull off the earrings and chuck them at the kitchen table. They skid into a pile of my dad's loose change. "Nowhere," I say. I yank my hair out of its bun and charge back up the stairs. A minute later, I've got my coat and I'm out the door.

Whenever I want to disappear, I head to the totem park. It's so quiet and shady there it makes me feel like a ghost. On a rainy day like today, mist rises from the ground and the totem poles loom in their little clearings, silent and tall as trees. Each pole stands for a family or a house, like a headstone in a graveyard or a European coat of arms. It must've looked just the same hundreds of years ago, when Sitka was still called Shee-Atika and nobody lived here but the Tlingit Indians.

My earlobes still smart from yanking the earrings off. I rub them and the tingling starts to go away. My dad's right. I probably did look like a Christmas tree. It hurts now, Lucy, but he just saved you a lot of embarrassment at school tomorrow.

I'm halfway down the main path, trying to make myself believe it, when I hear a noise in the bushes. It's that stray again. She's following me.

I cross the picnic ground. She's behind me, at the edge of the clearing. She's a determined one, I'll give her that.

"You don't want my kind of trouble, dog," I tell her. "You're better off on the streets."

She just cocks her sandy head and listens, then follows me anyway, all the way back through the park and into town.

I don't want to go home just yet. I don't want to risk seeing my dad again. So I sit by the water and wait. The entire time, the stray sits with me. It's strange not to be alone.

When it gets too cold and dark to stay out any longer, I head back toward the house. That outfit was stupid anyway, I tell myself. And the jewelry was definitely overkill. I pretend not to notice, but the mutt is following me.

By the time I reach our yard, she's only a few feet behind me. I should keep going but I stop. I can't help it. I sit down on the curb and she joins me. She's got a limp and looks more than a little worn down. Her breath hangs in the air, just the same as mine.

"How am I going to take care of a dog?" I ask her. She just lowers her head and looks up at me.

I put my hand on the back of her neck and give her a pat. Her tail thumps the ground twice, so hard it sounds like a drum. I like this dog. With any luck she can live under the tarp in the yard and my dad will never know.

—/—

I have a dog. I slept well last night, even though my dad came home after midnight, sick and loud. I have a dog and she's all mine.

In the morning I pull on my fuzzy blue sweater and

an old pair of jeans and head to McDonald's with my new dog. I call her Santa Barbara because it matches the warm sandy color of her face and paws. It's a cumbersome name, I know, and I'll probably shorten it to Saint or Bar or something so she'll sound tougher than she looks. But I like it just the same. It's a foreign-sounding, California name, and just about as far away from Sitka as I can make it.

Bar waits for me outside while I read my requisite pages of *The Old Man and the Sea* over coffee with tons of sugar. For her patience I give Bar a couple of sausage muffins, courtesy of my dad's liquor-store change. It's the one thing that works between my dad and me. He dumps his cash on the kitchen table every night, right before he reaches for the bottle opener. In the morning I get breakfast and I'm happy.

Outside the school, I give Bar a farewell scratch under the chin. "Wish me luck." She watches me walk to the door before trotting away.

The "photo shoot" is set up in the auditorium first thing in the morning. Sheila is already there, wearing pink rhinestones. "Aren't they neat? My mom got them for me at the mall in Juneau. I was going to wear the ring, too, but it won't show in the picture and it's kind of big on me, so why bother?" Everybody is dressed up for the yearbook shoot except for me.

"That's a nice sweater. . . ." Sheila trails off, picking at a stray fuzzball or two. She doesn't notice the dog hair.

"Yeah, it's dark," I reply. Inside, I'm praying for this to all end soon. Everyone else is dressed to impress. Charlotte Baker and her flunky, Tina, waltz by in full makeup, hair done up in flouncy buns with even the stray short pieces curled. They take one look at my tent-sized sweater and burst out giggling.

"Don't trip on the way out, Charlotte," Sheila chirps after them. "Shame to leave your face print in the snow!"

That snags a laugh out of me, and Sheila gives me a high five. Then, all too soon, it's my turn to sit in front of the camera.

My sweater is hot and itchy under the photo lights. I'm starting to wish I'd worn flannel. At least then I'd feel more human.

The photographer adjusts his lights and takes a look through his camera.

"Smile," he says. I do.

"Wait a minute." He frowns and turns a knob and raises the camera on its tripod. "Okay, now." He takes a look. And adjusts the tripod again. Finally he cranks it as high as it can go and has to grab a chair to stand on just to see through the viewfinder.

By the time the bulb flashes, I'm not smiling. But the photographer's all grins. "We'll put you in the last row when it's time for the group shot," he says brightly. I want to smash him into dirt. Instead, I say, "Thanks," and lamely step aside for the next kid.

After school Bar is waiting for me again at the end of the block. Her tail thumps when she sees me. But before I can reach her, Tina Martin and Charlotte Baker shove past me. "Who put the mountain on the sidewalk?" Charlotte yaps. "Oh, sorry, Giant," she and Tina sing in unison.

I want to pound them into the ground. But I don't have to. Bar is on them in a second like a mad dog, fur bristling, barking for all she's worth.

Charlotte and Tina scream like the little twits they are and run into the street to get away from her. Bar barks until they get to the other side and disappear down the block. Me, I'm on the ground laughing. I can't stop, even when Bar starts licking my face. We roll around like pups and I swear a dog can laugh too.

When I recover enough to walk again, we stroll through the totem park and I tell her how the pictures went. It's funny. I should feel as miserable as I know I'm going to look in my picture. The thing is, I don't feel bad at all. I feel . . . normal.

Huh. That's a new one.

Bar gives me a look like she's saying it's high time.

Then she spots a bird nearby and trots off to investigate. A normal dog with a normal kid.

"Normal." I try the word on for size. But it's like trying on this sweater in front of my tiny mirror. I can't tell if it fits.

CHAPTER 3

January 31

SITKA, ALASKA

"What's gotten into you lately?" Sheila catches me by surprise in the lunchroom. I scramble to hide the book in my hands.

"What do you mean?"

"You *know* what I mean," she says, exasperated. She plunks her tray down across from mine. "Two weeks, Lucy. For two weeks something's made you all happy, and I want to know what."

I shrug and try to look innocent. "Nothing. Just the usual."

And I have a dog. But I don't mention that part. Santa Barbara is all mine. For two weeks now, to the day. We eat breakfast together, and dinner, and never ever let each other feel lonely. Bar doesn't care if my dad comes home drunk, or wakes up drunk, or simply ignores me. She just thumps her tail and follows me out the side door without telling the whole town that Joe Otsego is a bum. And she doesn't seem to care that I'm five and a half feet taller than her, or that my shadow blocks out the sun when she's next to me. She makes me happy. I guess it shows.

Sheila narrows her eyes at me. "Wait a minute. What's that sticking up there?" Before I can yank it away, she snatches my copy of *The Old Man and the Sea* from me—along with the college brochures I have tucked inside.

"University of Alaska? Aha!" she exclaims. Then it registers. Her eyes go wide. "Wow, you serious? You want to go to college?"

"Yeah, maybe." I try to sound casual, but I'm too excited. "I thought about what you said. Maybe I could get a scholarship."

"Oh, absolutely!" Sheila claps her hands. "You just need a few extracurricular things too, you know? Like sports or drama or—" Sheila is all lit up now. She waves the pamphlets in the air like winning lottery tickets. "Wow. College! I thought it was just a boy or something. But college is way better."

She riffles through the catalogs. "Hey. You've got UC Santa Barbara in here too. Great! We could go to school together . . . *if* I get in. Crap. What if I don't get in? Wait—what if *you* take the last scholarship? Then I'll never get to go!"

I take back the brochures, my ears turning red. "I only said I was looking into it."

Sheila slumps down and gives me a wry smile. "Sorry, Luce. Didn't mean to sound like a jealous jerk. You're a shoo-in, is all. And it would be cool to be roommates or something." She gets a dreamy look on her face and her eyes float down to my tray.

"Jeez, Luce, got enough food on there?" I'm usually a big eater, but lately I've been really piling it on at the cafeteria. Today I've got two plates stacked high with three cheeseburgers, two hot dogs, and some purple slop for dessert. It's cheaper than dog food for Bar, even though it tastes about the same. "Are you sure everything's okay?" Sheila asks, fixing me with a look.

"Never better."

"Well, if you don't want me to know, there's nothing I can say, I guess. . . ." She gives an exaggerated sigh and peels the wrapper off her straw. "*Is* there something going on?"

Of course there is something going on. Bar. But I'm not ready to share her with Sheila or anyone else. Strange as it sounds, I've started to think that if a stray dog can find a home and make good, maybe a stray kid can too. So I'm looking into college—just looking. All I know for sure is Bar's the best thing that's ever happened to me. The thought of Sheila cooing and *awwing* over her makes me kind of jealous. For now I just want to keep her to myself.

So I return Sheila's look with a shrug. "I need to eat. I'm a growing girl."

"Hardee har har," Sheila laughs, and swats me on the arm. "Fine, keep your secrets. Mysterious Lucy the Giant—doesn't let me over, doesn't let me in, doesn't tell me anything. I swear, you can be so frustrating sometimes."

I don't know what to say to this, so I just say nothing, which makes her even madder. I don't actually have many secrets. I mean, I can pretend the whole town doesn't know about my mom and my dad, but they do. Bar is the only real secret I have left. She's the best one. Maybe secrets, real or not, are what keeps Sheila and me from really being friends in the end.

"Well, I gotta go," I say, switching subjects. Sheila frowns but leaves it alone. I grab a sandwich bag from the counter and stuff the rest of the food from my tray into it. Sheila wrinkles her nose but doesn't say anything more about it.

"See ya in study hall," she says, and heads for the door.

But I'm not going to study hall today. Instead, I'm going to go check on Bar.

When the bell rings, I slip outside behind the

school and whistle. No answer. Bar doesn't come charging out of the trees, tail wagging. I whistle again. A low whimper comes from behind the sports shed. "Bar?"

There she is, wedged between the shed and the school building.

"You okay, Bar?" I crouch down. She thumps her tail on the ground.

"C'mon, girl, c'mon." I coax her out with little kissing sounds and a piece of hot dog from my lunch bag. Bar wags her tail a little and shuffles into the open, but she doesn't eat the hot dog.

"What's the matter, pup? Not good enough?" I sniff the hot dog and wrinkle my nose. "I see what you mean. C'mon, Bar, we're going home early. I'll find something good for you to eat, promise."

There's only one more class left today. Normally, I'd rather stay—it's better than wandering the streets all afternoon. But Bar is more important. She's been looking a little beaten up lately. I think it's from sleeping out in the cold. I've been skipping breakfast all week to save enough cash for a little bed for her—another reason for the big lunches. But now, I think I'll use the money to take her to the vet instead, just for a checkup. Just in case.

I count my stash in my head. Nineteen dollars, including the change. That won't buy a doggie bed yet, let alone a trip to the vet. For the first time I wish Dad would buy more booze so I could have the change that much quicker. I know I could just ask him for the money, but he'd flip if he knew about Bar. Besides, I'd rather starve than ask my dad for help with this. Bar is completely mine.

At home, I do find something fairly good for Bar to eat—a can of chili, which is kind of like dog food, and some leftover fast-food chicken I strip off the bone. Still, she doesn't eat much. I sit there with her in the mudroom for a really long time, reading out loud to her from *The Old Man and the Sea*. She seems to like it and rests her head on my knee, listening. But then I hear the truck rattle into the driveway. My dad is home. I slip Bar out the side door and we do a quick dash to the boat tarp, where we can hide. I've even brought out a few extra blankets so she won't get so cold tonight.

"Phew, we made it," I tell her, and giggle, waiting for her to lick my face like she usually does when we run together. But this time, she doesn't pounce on me. Instead, she hunkers down and starts to pant like she's just run a marathon.

"Bar? Are you okay?" Oh, God. Her sides are heaving so hard she looks like she's going to pass out right there.

"Don't worry, sweetie, I'll get help." I don't want to leave her, but I run into the kitchen to call a vet, any vet. Nobody is open. I start to panic. Maybe she'll be okay if she can just get in from the cold, I think. So I wait for my dad to leave again, which he does as soon as happy hour hits. Then I sneak Bar into my bedroom and let her have the bed. I stay on the floor, wide awake all night, listening to her breathe. "It's going to be all right," I tell her, trying to sound calm. It seems to work for her. Me, I'm wide-eyed with worry into the wee hours of the morning. The only time I leave her is when Murph calls me down to the bar to pick up my dad.

When we get home, Bar is asleep. I watch over her until I can't stay awake anymore.

By morning she's gotten much, much worse. Forget school. I race down to the kitchen and grab the phone book again, dialing up the first animal hospital I see.

"Hello? Yes, my dog is sick. Can someone see her now? Great." I hesitate. "How . . . how much?"

I hang up the phone, numb. Fifty dollars just to look at her. I have nineteen. And another five in change my dad left on the table. But it isn't enough.

The only sound in the house is breathing—my dad, drunk and sleeping on the couch where I left him, and Bar, upstairs wheezing like an old accordion. She sounds horrible and I can't wait. I race upstairs and scoop her into my arms. Then I carry her down to the living room and pray that for once my dad will be the dad I need.

"Daddy?" He doesn't budge. I nudge him with my knee. "Dad, wake up. Dad!"

I shift Bar in my arms and start to shake him.

He rolls over and exhales a beery cloud into my face. Barely awake, he stares up at me, his eyes little slits in his stubbly face. "What?" he breathes.

"Dad, I need your help. Can I borrow thirty dollars? My dog is sick, Daddy. I think she's dying."

He doesn't say anything so I nudge him again. Bar's panting turns into long, slow drags. It scares me. I push my dad again. "Please, help me! Just this once." I shake and scream and sob at him.

It works. He rolls over. He sits up. And I see his face is purple, his eyes red with strain. He doesn't see me, but he knows exactly where I am.

"Daddy?"

He stands up, spit in the corner of his mouth, and raises his hand across his chest, ready to strike.

I run. I run the way I ran when I was three and he fought with my mother. I run through the mudroom, past the truck, into the trees, into the snow. Bar gasps in my arms.

The rages don't last long. They take too much out

of him. But Bar doesn't know that. I tell her so, and rock her, and rock myself, huddled in the snow the same way I was so long ago, the day my mother left for good. It's been seven years, but the cold in the pit of my stomach makes it feel like yesterday.

My mother came from a little town outside of Kake, which is already a little town. A pissy little place, she told me. Lots of drunks. Lots of mean drunks. I looked it up once at school. Almost every month somebody dies in my mom's hometown in a barroom brawl. More bars than jobs, I guess.

She must've thought she'd left that behind when she came to Sitka and met my dad. But she just married into it instead. After she left, my dad told people she'd gone back to her family. Couldn't handle life on the better side of the tracks. But she wanted a better life for her daughter, if not for herself. That's why she left me behind. A drunk who yells is better than a drunk who hits, I guess.

I know that's the story my dad told the social services people when he started collecting unemployment. What I don't know is if it's true.

Maybe I hid too well that day and she couldn't find me. Maybe she didn't care. Or maybe she couldn't save me, the way I'm trying to save Bar. Maybe she just didn't try. "I'm not like her, Bar," I whisper into

Bar's ear. "I'll save you. I promise. I won't leave you here."

Twenty minutes later, shaking from more than the cold, with Bar still wheezing in my arms, I creep back into the house. I shoulder my backpack and scan the living room for my dad's jacket. It's lying beside him at the foot of the sofa. He's out cold. He doesn't move when I go through his pockets. Or when I shut the door behind us, my fist around one of his credit cards and twenty dollars in cash.

I try to get Bar into the passenger side of the truck. She doesn't whimper. She's putting all her effort into breathing. I put mine into opening the door. But it's locked and I don't have the key. I scrape the frost off the window. My dad's locked them inside. So I hoist Bar higher into my arms and jog as fast as I can without hurting her to the doctor's office.

The rain turned to snow during the night. It should be peaceful, that soft blanket of silence I was hoping for. But now it just makes Bar's breathing seem louder, more ragged. The snow is ugly.

Slipping on the icy pavement, my arms aching from the effort of being gentle—something I never worried about when I carried my dad—I finally reach the doctor's office. It's a low-slung, trailer-like building. I can't reach the door handle with my arms around Bar, so I pound on the wall beside the door with my foot until someone opens it up for me.

All I can see is the woman behind the front desk. Her mouth hangs open in shock. I don't care. I rest Bar on the countertop.

"Please . . . I called earlier—"

"It's okay, dear. You can put her down on that bench over there. The doctor will be free in a moment."

"Okay, okay." I nod, but I don't move. The woman seems to understand.

"Have you been to see us before?"

"No. No. I just . . . got her."

The woman's eyes flicker over my face. She's new in town. She doesn't know me.

"Okay, well, I just need you to fill this out before the doctor can get started."

I feel like screaming. Why is everything moving so slowly? My hands shake, and I can't hold the pen.

"Look, on the phone you said fifty dollars. Can't I just pay and have you look at her now? Please?"

The assistant looks at the papers in front of me. My hand's shaking so badly I can't sign my own name. She closes her mouth at last and, for the first time, looks at Bar. Bar's breath rattles in her chest.

"Cash or credit?"

I hand her the card. "My dad said to charge it. He's back at home."

She hesitates only slightly, then runs it through.

"I'm sorry. It was declined."

"What?" I say softly. Bar whimpers on the countertop. I can't even cry. "What?"

The vet's assistant gives me a look then, the same look Vickie Drake gave me from behind the counter at McDonald's. Seven kinds of pity. Only this woman isn't a local. If she was, she'd know who I am. She'd have given me that look a whole lot sooner.

"Don't worry. I'll just do it the other way," she says to me confidentially, and runs it through the imprint machine instead.

"Thank you," I say in that same quieter-than-quiet voice.

"I'll go get Dr. Perkins." She goes through the double doors. I carry Bar to the bench and hold her with her head in my lap, humming the tune to a song whose words I can't remember. She pants in low, deep drags and looks up at me with those giant eyes. Please, God, I think, don't let me be too late. Please let her be okay.

"We'll take her now." The assistant is back with a gurney, but I won't let Bar go. A man stands in a lab coat behind the woman. Dr. Perkins. Another out-of-towner I don't know. He shakes my hand, like he would an adult's.

"Ma'am, please just have a seat," he tells me, and comes forward to pick Bar up out of my arms. "We'll take a look at her and then I'll come talk to you. Okay?"

I can't speak. I just nod and never stop looking at Bar as they wheel her away. She died on the gurney before he could even look at her.

The vet says it looked like parvo or some sort of worm. It had gotten to her heart. And then he tells me that should teach me a lesson about hanging around with strays.

Not the kind of thing you say to a kid who's just lost her best friend. But I don't tell him that. I'm barely listening. All I know is that Bar is dead.

I cry over Bar's body for two hours before they take her away to be cremated. They'll send me the ashes in a tin can, they say, because I can't afford the urn. They'll send her ashes to my house.

But I won't be there. I can't make myself go back.

I never want to see my father again. All the days I picked up his bottles and wiped up his messes. All the nights I went out in the snow to carry him home. I tried to take care of him, but he's still a drunk. I tried to take care of Bar, and she's still dead. I am not Lucy the Giant, the Amazon from Sitka. I'm a failure. Maybe my mother knew I would be, the way she knew my dad would never change. Maybe that's why she left us both behind.

—/—

I wander the streets for a long time, hoping to get cold enough to stop feeling hurt. But the cold doesn't help. I can't seem to walk far enough. Bar is gone.

Finally I cross the bridge to Japonski Island and follow the little two-lane road to the airport. It's one terminal, really, and a few hangars, corrugated-tin shacks. But inside the terminal it's warm, and the airport diner is the only place open this late, besides McDonald's. If I go to McDonald's, I might see my dad. I would rather die.

I slip into a booth at the restaurant and nod when the guy behind the bar comes around with a menu. "Get you something? Slice of pie?"

I shake my head and sit there, stunned.

Did my mother feel this way just before she left us? I can almost understand running from this kind of pain. My brain is spinning with everything I've lost. For just a few days I had imagined a life outside Sitka, away from my dad. For one brief moment I could imagine being happy. One moment too long.

Grow up, my dad would probably say, if he said

anything at all. Take it like a man. The way he took my mother's leaving. Like a fish to water. Like a drunk to a bottle. Maybe that's the answer to numbing the pain.

"Hey, lady," the guy behind the bar calls out. "Your plane's leaving."

It takes me a minute to realize he's talking to me. "What?"

He polishes a glass with a rag. "You're with the work tour, right? Well, your charter's leaving. Not another plane to Kodiak for at least a day."

My backpack must look like luggage to him. Like the stuff all the college students carry when they come to Alaska to get rich in the canneries. And just like the vet and his assistant, this guy doesn't know me. Doesn't know Lucy the Giant. All he sees is a grown woman on her way out of town.

And suddenly I see it too. A way out.

"Thank you," I say, and I mean it.

The plane is a small one. Thirty other people, all at least five years older than me, standing on the tarmac waiting to board. Five years older, but we look the same. Maybe no one will notice until I reach Kodiak. Maybe no one will notice me ever again. I'm going where Lucy the Giant doesn't exist. Lucy the kid with the dead stray for a pet. I'm going north. If I've got to grow up, then I'm going to do it fast.

CHAPTER 4

February 1

KODIAK, ALASKA

Kodiak is cold as a bitch. And icy, too. We come in on a little plane that lets you feel every rip and bump in the sky. I see snowfields and water, glaciers and more ice. Bar would have loved it here. She'd have run wild until she froze to death out in the snow. Anything would've been better than that metal gurney back in Sitka. No snow could ever be that cold.

It's not until we land and the door flies open that I realize I have no idea what I'm going to do. "Cross the tarmac to the terminal and a bus'll bring you into town," the pilot says, flinging the door open. I grab my pack and shuffle out with everybody else.

The terminal is even smaller than the little hallway we call an airport in Sitka. This is more like a shack. I'm a little nervous that someone will check IDs or something when we board the bus, but if they were being careful, they'd have done that back on the plane, I guess.

I sit up front so I can see where we're going, but hunch down into a corner as best I can. The frigid air seeps through the bus windows and reminds me how far I am from home. I'm starting to get scared. The bus hauls off and creeps its way along a crusty old road with nothing but trees for a little while. Suddenly someone behind me says, "Home, sweet home," and I realize we're there.

I can't say much for Kodiak. There are docks, but not the pleasure docks like we have at the harbor in Sitka. Beneath the gloomy lamplight rows of working boats clang against each other on the shoreline. Opposite the water the town sprawls across the hills in grays and whites. Even the buildings here look cold.

"If you got a job, go to work. Otherwise, hotel's down the street," the driver announces, and parks the bus in a way that tells me it's for the night. Around me, the other seasonal workers start to shuffle, rouse themselves, and head off to what must be familiar territory. But not me.

I can feel the tears well in my eyes, hot and unwelcome. Buck up, Lucy girl, I tell myself. Stay low and stay out of the way. My little mantra chimes in like a bell and I realize nothing has changed. Kodiak is like any other town. I climb off the bus into the cold and brace myself against the wind for a few minutes, looking for the familiar gleam of neon that signifies a bar. Suddenly I see it, and I know exactly where I'll spend the night.

—/—

The Polar Bar is the same on the inside as any of my dad's favorite hangouts, which means lots of booze and, more importantly, a warm stockroom where the drunks can sleep it off. I press through the heavy door and let it swing shut behind me. Immediately the dim light and the scent of spilled draft and sweat hit me. As the guy on the bus said, home, sweet home. The bartender looks up but doesn't even card me. I'm an adult now, remember? I try to act like one, and stride into the room.

For my plan to work I need to order at least one drink. Something strong enough to make them think I'm wasted. I stagger just a bit as I head toward the bar. Hopefully the bartender will think I've already got a head start.

"Jameson's," I mumble, remembering a name from one of the bottles at home. A tiny glass is splashed in front of me. I remember this smell. I remember hating it.

"Thanks." I grab it and dive for a table in the

corner. If I make him think I'm running a tab, I won't have to spend what little cash I have just yet.

Once I'm safely seated in the corner, I take a look around.

The place is crowded. As crowded as any place, I suppose, in a town of ten thousand. It's packed full of men, some of them even bigger than me, all smelling faintly of fish, and women, all smaller than me, who smell like perfume or like the men they're with. The clock on the wall says it's Miller Time, which also looks like nine-thirty. I'm exhausted, but it's too early to get any sleep and hope to pass it off as a blackout. So I sit there and I start to think of Bar. When that starts to hurt too much, I switch to eavesdropping instead. An actual adult would be making plans, I realize, if she was really going to stay. Maybe if I listen long enough, something will come up.

The talk is about work—who's leaving on what boat, when the crabbing season will start, et cetera. A few of the people sound like they flew in on the same plane I did. And they are looking hard for work.

"Maybe Old Man Thomas has a spot," one guy suggests. He looks like he's been around a few times, and pulled under more than once. "But I wouldn't recommend it. Man's a menace to society."

The people around him grunt in agreement and raise their glasses.

The place is getting really full now. The room is hot with wool sweaters rubbing back to back. I'm lucky I was able to find a table to myself.

It doesn't last long.

"'Scuse me." A man with a scraggly, tobacco-stained beard pulls out one of the chairs across from me and waves at three of his friends. "Over here, four of 'em. Got 'em."

Crap, I think. My little ploy will be a lot harder to pull off with a crowd. What's more, I'll have to talk to them. I'm so tired and nervous I start to tremble. Get a grip, Lucy. At the bar two of the three friends, a short, middle-aged woman and a young, thin rail of a guy, start to come over. The fourth, a man in a deep blue parka, waves them off without turning around.

"Harley's in a sulk," the woman says, joining the table. In her hands are a beer and a shot glass of something nasty-looking. She nods in my direction by way of a hello.

Trying to emulate my dad, I simply grunt and sip a tiny bit of my Jameson's. Immediately I start to cough and hack. For all the booze I grew up around, I never developed much of a taste for it.

"Hey, buddy, take it easy!" the bearded guy says, and pours me some water from a pitcher.

"That ain't no guy, Don," the younger one says.

"Yeah, 'cause they grow women that big in Alaska," Don replies sarcastically.

The woman at the table snorts, trying not to chuckle. "Sorry, Don, I think he's right. Isn't he, hon?"

There seems to be no way out of this conversation, but I try. I let my eyes close just a smidgen. Maybe they'll think I'm sleeping. But that never works, not in school when you forget your homework, not at home when your dad's on a bender. And it doesn't work here, either.

"Hey, maybe you can help us, ma'am," the young guy starts in. "Maybe you can help us settle an argument."

I shake my head. "Don't want any trouble," I mumble, the way I've heard my dad say a million times. But trouble's what he always got.

"Naw, it ain't gonna be no trouble," he goes on. "It's just that we're waking a buddy here. We lost a comrade-at-arms and we're having us a little wake."

"I'm sorry." And I am sorry. I guess I'm waking Bar, too. So maybe it's not so bad to be with people right now. The little group falls silent, and the young guy lifts his glass toward the center of the table. "To Monroe, man. He fought the good fight."

"Amen," says the old guy, Don.

"*L'chaim,*" says the woman, and they drink. I take

a sip of my water too, and say a silent prayer for Bar. I hope she forgives me for not saving her. I hope she forgives me for being too late.

"What's your name, friend?" Don asks.

I don't know if it's because I'm thinking about her, or because I'm scared. "Bar," I say quickly. "Barbara."

"Well, Bar-Barbara, I'm Don. This is Tracer, and the lady is Geneva. We work off the *Miranda Lee*. Monroe was part of our crew."

"Monroe crewed with *me* longer than any of you, on the *Gonakadet*," Tracer says. His eyes glint in the bar light and I know, despite the one beer he's nursing, that he's drunk already.

"And therein lies the argument," Geneva says, tossing back the vile-looking shot. Her blond bob bounces with every move of her head. She winks at me and I'm reminded of a fairy godmother.

"Monroe left behind a few personal effects, and no will or testament," she explains. "The most valuable item being a survival suit he never even got to use." I have no idea what a survival suit is, but I nod anyway.

"Bastard wave rolled right on top of us before we knew it." Don swears under his breath. "It's a wonder Harley was able to pull any of us out in time. I don't know why I keep putting up with this bull."

Stay low, stay out of the way, I know, but I just can't help myself. "What happened? What happened to Monroe?"

Instantly I'm sorry I said anything. Easiest way not to look like an adult, ask a stupid kiddie question. Then wait for them to blow the whistle. The trio blinks back at me silently for a few moments.

"Heck, man, what happens to most of us, eventually. You make a mistake, you go under. Ain't nothin' but the good Lord gonna stop you," Don finally says with a cackle.

Geneva seems to sniff back a tear, and the young guy, Tracer, he starts to look sulky and hunkers down into his sweater. It's a look I recognize. Tracer is brewing for a fight.

"That damn survival suit's mine by rights," he mutters. "Monroe gave it to me before he died."

"Now, Tracer, everybody knows Harley owns that suit. He gives it to whoever he wants. Monroe owed him, and that don't barely pay off his funeral," Don chides him.

"Well then, why the hell doesn't *Har*-ley come over here and drink with us? Why doesn't he come over here and—"

"Give you the suit?" Geneva asks with a raised eyebrow. She reaches out a hand and pats my arm confidentially. I'm losing my grip on anonymity by the minute. "Tracer here thinks he can get that suit out of Harley while he's in his cups. Harley's a poker face, for sure, unless he's been at it. But Harley hasn't touched a bottle in over a year. Get used to it, Tracer. And get over it too."

"Hell, Geneva," Tracer whines—I'm already starting not to like him—"the least he could do is come over here and drink with us like we're all crewmates or something."

Geneva shrugs like she's giving up. "Why don't you ask him?"

"I think I will," Tracer says evenly. He stands up, leans his palms on the tabletop, and hollers toward the bar, "Harley, come on over! Harley, it's time for a toast!"

Apparently Harley doesn't think so. No one at the bar turns around. Not even the bartender. Tracer must be known for shouting across rooms or something, because I'm the only one who flinches at all.

"Oh, well." Don shrugs. Geneva starts to chuckle.

"Shut up!" Tracer shouts at them. "I'm not gonna let him make a fool of me."

"Then sit down," Geneva recommends.

"Too late," Don says at the same time. But Tracer's on a mission. He shoves past them to the bar and grabs someone by the shoulder. The man in the blue parka, the one they came in with. This must be Harley.

"What do you want, Tracer?" Harley asks. He's barely speaking above a whisper, but the room's gotten so quiet I can hear every word he says. I catch my breath. Tracer seems to know he's outclassed and loses some of his bravado.

"Nothin', Harley. Just wanted you to have a drink with us. A drink to Monroe, 's all."

Harley raises a glass of water. "Already had one," he replies in that same low voice.

"Jesus, Harley, can't you just be civil? Steal a man's property after driving him into the storm that kills him, and now you won't even drink with the crew!" Tracer shouts, sounding just like a little kid throwing a tantrum.

Harley's broad shoulders heave with a sigh. "You want the survival suit that bad, Tracer, you can earn it."

Tracer shifts from foot to foot, trying not to show his excitement. "Really? How?"

"Same way Monroe got it in the first place. A contest."

"Contest?" Mumbles go up throughout the bar. Looks like everyone is in the mood for a contest. For the time being I forget about not having a place to sleep and wait to see what happens next.

"What kind of contest?" Tracer says nervously.

"This is a bar, Tracer," Don chimes in. "What else? A drinking contest."

Tracer instantly seems to relax. "Oh, sure. Let's go."

"Not against me." Harley shakes his head. He almost says "moron," I'm sure of it. "You drink against anyone else who wants Monroe's survival suit." He surveys the bar. "Any takers?"

The only taker is a broomstick-thin older man sitting at one of the tables. "I'll give it a go," he bellows. But then he stands up and the bar erupts in laughter—the poor guy is shorter than my dad.

"Man, you wouldn't fit in the *elbow* of Monroe's suit. Even Tracer here's gonna have to stuff it some," Don laughs from our table. "This young lady here has a better shot at it than you!"

I'm so shocked I do exactly what I shouldn't. I stand up and back away. Or more precisely, I stand up and tower over the table. Don and Geneva look up at me funny.

"Sweet Jesus," Don whispers. "I was right."

My eyes grow wide. "N-no way, mister," I stammer. But now the whole bar's looking at me and I don't know what a grown-up would do. I'm pretty sure they wouldn't back down. But . . .

"That's it?" Tracer squeaks. "I gotta go up against *her*?"

A cheer goes up from the bar and the next thing I know, a bunch of people are peeling me off the wall and plopping me down at a table across from Tracer. At the bar Harley turns around to watch us. I get a glimpse of sharp blue eyes before a very large bottle blocks my view.

"Tequila!" the bartender announces, and I'm reminded of those monster truck races on cable—the Crushinator meets the Scared-As-Crapinator. Staying low and out of the way never sounded so good, or seemed so incredibly hard. Lucy girl, what have you gotten yourself into?

"First one under the table loses. First one to get sick loses. First one to pass out loses. A shot a turn."

Two glasses are poured and the warm, sickening smell of booze floods my nose. It smells like my dad. A little whitish thing bobs in the bottom of the bottle. With a hot flush I realize it's a worm. I might get sick before this thing is even started.

Geneva whispers in my ear. "Do this thing, Barb, and I'll guarantee you a spot on the *Miranda Lee*. You *are* looking for work, like everyone else out here?"

I nod. A job? I could get an honest-to-goodness

job just by drinking? Obviously I'm having a better run of luck than my dad ever did.

"Here we go!" Tracer hoots like a monkey and slams down his first drink. All eyes turn to me. I pray I'm the only one who sees my hands trembling as I pick up my glass. But before I tilt it down my throat, I see Harley watching me. His eyes are so intense I forget myself. I mean to sip my tequila, but it's gone in one gulp. My throat burns and I cough. Everyone laughs.

"Water," I croak.

"No time for water, little lady," Tracer hollers, and slams another drink before sliding the next one to me.

I'm starting to hate Tracer. I glance around for Harley again and he winks at me. Now my face is getting hot. I choke down the second glass. By the third I can't feel my tongue anymore. My whole body is glowing and I'm smiling like an idiot. But somewhere underneath it all I feel horribly, horribly ill. I'm not supposed to be doing this. I'm not supposed to be like this. But then I think of Bar and how horrible life is without her. Who cares anymore? Why try to be good when all it gets me is down? I toss back another drink without batting an eye. I can't say the same for Tracer.

They say that alcohol brings out your true

personality—some people are happy drunks, some are sloppy, some are affectionate. And some are jerks, like my dad. I guess I'm a sad drunk, because by the time they take away the bottle, I feel so blue I never want to see another glass of tequila—or another sunrise, for that matter. I just want to put my head on the table and disappear.

But instead, I get hauled to my feet, slapped on the back, hugged, whooped and hollered at, and congratulated.

"Jesus, Barbara, I never seen someone pack it away like that," Don shouts gleefully. "Tracer went under three shots ago and we couldn't stop you!"

"We've all got demons, I guess," Harley says, coming up to me. My face grows even hotter and I know I must be the color of a tomato. I look away.

"Congratulations, I suppose." He looks me over. "You can pick up the suit tomorrow. *Miranda Lee*, slip fourteen. Catch you all in the morning," he tells his crew, and leaves the bar.

The strength drains from my legs. I collapse onto a bench that creaks dangerously beneath me.

"Whoa!" Geneva exclaims, trying to steady me. "We need to get this lady a place to stay."

"I don't think she's going anywhere, Geneva." Don puts an arm around me. "Sparky?" he shouts to the bartender. And then everything goes black.

CHAPTER 5

February 2

KODIAK, ALASKA

Bar is licking my face. At least that's what it feels like. "Cut it out." I chuckle and try to push her away. My hands get tangled in her fur, which is stringy and wet for some reason. Then she shouts, "Hey!" And I open my eyes. Two things come to me at once: Bar is dead, and I'm petting a mop.

"What?" I sit up and realize I'm exactly where I wanted to be last night—on the stockroom floor of the Polar Bar. But instead of a fake buzz, I've got a very real headache and my mouth tastes like acid.

Above the mop is a guy who's obviously seen it all. "Coffee's out front. Then you'll want the *Miranda Lee*. Harbor's across the street. Can't miss it."

It takes me a minute to realize what the heck he's talking about, and then I remember—the contest. I won.

"Thanks." I rise unsteadily to my feet. Before I'm halfway up, the guy is in my face wearing a grin that shows his three gold teeth.

"Didja really drink that snot-nosed Tracer under the table and keep going?"

I nod, even though I'm not sure *what* happened last night.

"Hoo, boy! That's gotta burn his butt. He'll never live it down. Outdone by a woman, and a greenhorn, too!"

He slaps his thigh, the sound ringing unnaturally loud in the little stockroom. My head is throbbing, so I don't wait for any more percussive moves. I grab a paper cup of black coffee and stumble outside into the bright white Kodiak morning. Safe on the street, I look down and can't figure out why, until I realize I'm looking for Bar. But she's never going to be waiting for me outside the Polar Bar or McDonald's or anywhere else. You're on your own, Lucy girl.

The wind leaves my sails. I plop down on a bench a few stores away from the bar and take stock of my situation. It's not that early anymore. The streets are peppered with people, mostly fishermen, gathering supplies and gossip. I sip my coffee slowly and close my eyes. What am I doing here? Day two, and I have a new problem—figuring out the next step. Since I don't seem to be coming up with any bright ideas, I decide to do as I'm told and head down to the harbor to find the *Miranda Lee*.

Kodiak is not a big town. Now, in the cold light of day, I can see things a bit more clearly. As the guy in the bar said, the town seems to be primarily built on this front street facing the harbor. Houses climb the back hills—the same cat-on-a-bathtub-ledge look as Sitka, but not so big, and more functional somehow. Sitka is for tourists. No doubt about it, Kodiak is a working town.

Even the harbor is like and unlike Sitka's, where I used to sit out the afternoons. Sitka's is full of pleasure boats, tall sails and lightweight fishing chairs. Next to Sitka, Kodiak looks like a demolition derby. Processing plants dot the far edges of the harbor, big floating versions of the cannery my dad works in, when he works at all. The bulk of the harbor slips are full this time of year with crabbing vessels—scarred, battered, and tough as heck. Their decks are piled high with heavy traps, and the boats themselves are bigger than the ones we have in Sitka. These are the kind that go for king crab on the open sea, not the little Dungeness we get in southeastern Alaska.

I'm not alone on the docks this morning. Other people are out making the rounds, hunting for work, being turned away. Hungover as I am, I can't even begin to compete. I close my eyes against the morning light and take a deep breath. A step at a time, Lucy girl. Just don't try to drink your way into another place to sleep tonight. You'd never survive this again.

"There she is!" a muffled voice announces as I reach slip 14, the resting place of the *Miranda Lee*.

She's nowhere near the biggest boat in the harbor, maybe fifty feet or so. Some of the others out here are three times that size. A little cabin takes up a full third of the *Miranda Lee*'s front deck. Two masts angle out from the sides of the cabin, rigged with pulleys and giant hooks. The rest of the deck is stacked with giant crab pots that look kind of like collapsed Slinkys lined with nets.

With her name scrawled across the stern in fading red letters and a little tired-looking flag in the same color atop the slanted wheelhouse, the *Miranda Lee* is not beautiful, but there is something inviting about her. The old guy from last night—Don, I think—clambers above deck in his bib pants, and waves.

"I knew you'd make it! Told Bobby at the bar to send you down, just in case. Tracer's gonna love this!"

I smile weakly. Somehow I've gotten in the middle of some sort of personal vendetta against Tracer. I look back the way I came, but I still have nowhere better to be.

"Geneva!" Don hollers over the side of the boat. "Guess who came to collect?"

I rock back on my heels silently as Geneva hauls herself over the side of the boat, where she's been trying to touch up the faded hull. Her hands are covered in white paint. She smiles at me and I can't help smiling back.

"Well, I'll be. Glad you made it, Barbara."

I blink. It takes me a minute to figure out who Barbara is. Oh, right. Me.

"Well, I didn't really . . . the guy at the bar . . ." I shut up. Stumbling around like this is only going to give me away. Low and out of the way, I remind myself.

"Well, hold on," Geneva says. "I'll fetch Harley. He'll want to give you the suit personally. But while you're here, I've got to ask—do you need the suit? I mean, do you have a situation already? Didn't you say you were looking for work?"

I hesitate, and I know I look like a fish gasping for air.

Don rubs his bald spot. "Shoot, Barb, what she means to say is, it ain't easy to find work up here, especially for a woman. But we've met you and we like what you got. If you're up for it, we'll put in a good word for you with the boss." I know I should answer, but I don't know what to say, so I just nod. I'm in shock. Getting a job can't be this easy. What happened to all the stuff Sheila said, about being too young, being a kid— But I'm not Lucy the Kid Giant anymore. I'm Barbara the adult. Barbara the soon-to-be crabber. Barbara the—

"Morning." Harley comes out on deck and tips his wool cap at me. My confidence disappears completely.

"Morning." My palms break into a sweat and I have to look down to avoid those piercing eyes.

"Hey, boss," Don cuts in. "Geneva and I were just talking, and Barbara here seems like she might be pretty handy to have around. Good with the pots and all."

"Is that so?" Harley says in a way that makes me look back up at him again, and just as quickly look away. This time, my eyes land on Geneva, and I see nothing but encouragement there.

"You ever crabbed before?"

No, sir, I start to say. But an adult wouldn't say that, would they? "No," I finally reply. "Not the way you mean."

Harley chuckles and I cringe. I just stepped in it somehow, I know. "The way *I* mean? What other way is there?"

"String and a garbage can off the shore. I do it all the time . . . uh, did, I mean, when I was a kid."

"Hey, I did that too," Geneva chimes in. "We all did. First sign of the crabbing bug, you know?"

"Right," Harley says. "Well, hold on and I'll get your suit." He disappears into the wheelhouse.

"Now, that went well," Don says.

I shake my head. "It was a disaster!"

"Just hold on there, Barb." Geneva winks at me. "Harley likes you."

"But . . ." It's like everyone here speaks a different language—Adult. I'm stuck.

I stand there nervously shifting from foot to foot, listening to the scraping sounds as Geneva swings over the railing and goes back to work. Overhead a couple of bald eagles swing wide circles and screech at each other in their squeaky-bicycle-tire voices. Cold as it is, I'm starting to sweat. Down the dock the crowd of job seekers is dwindling, but not by much. Mostly they seem to be giving up. No jobs to be had. Halibut Hut, here I come.

And then Harley stalks out of the wheelhouse empty-handed. He squints at me sideways, then looks away. I manage to look at him when he finally speaks. "Listen," he says, rubbing the back of his sunburned neck with a square hand, "if you want a job, you got it. We need an extra hand with the pots. Geneva'll show you the ropes. Just stay low and stay—"

"—out of the way," I finish for him. Harley nods and walks away. My whole body is tingling. It's like my guardian angel just channeled through Harley and said, Lucy girl, this is it. Hold on with both hands and don't let go.

The most profound moment of my life is shattered by a whoop and a holler. Don scrambles over to me.

"Yeehaw!" he shouts, and slaps me on the back. "Three against one again! The odds are in our favor!"

"What do you mean?" I try not to sound panicked. Geneva pats my arm.

"Don't worry about him, honey. He and Tracer are at each other all the time." I wince and she quickly adds, "Aw, they're harmless. And nothing a woman like you probably hasn't handled before."

I try to look knowing and nod.

"Well then, crewman, where's your stuff?"

I show her my backpack.

"Easy enough. But you'll need supplies. Give me a minute to wash up and I'll give you the nickel tour, then we'll hit the shore." She disappears into the wheelhouse.

"Catch ya later." Don smiles at me. "Tracer's gonna love this!"

Suddenly I'm alone on the deck of my new home, completely flummoxed by what has just occurred. For one thing, I know absolutely nothing about crabbing. Only that it's hard work, you get practically no sleep, and boats can go out for a month at a time without coming back to shore.

What am I getting into? I haven't been on a boat, outside of a ferry, since I was a little kid. I feel like I'm about to take a final exam I forgot to study for. The bow is front, I remind myself. The stern is back. Starboard is right, port is left. My head hurts. At least I don't get seasick. That would be a hard one to explain.

I scratch my head under my woolen cap and sit down on a coil of rope to wait for Geneva's return.

"What the hell're *you* doing here?" somebody shouts at me from the pier. I don't need to turn around to know that it's Tracer. This time I decide to simply stay quiet and see what happens.

"I know you hear me." Tracer clambers on board the boat and drops an armload of groceries.

"I don't know what game you were playing last night, but I know you cheated. That suit's mine fair and square. It wasn't Harley's to gamble away in the first place."

He's in my face now, so I have to look at him. I decide to do so standing up. Tracer's face falls, as if he'd forgotten, until now, that I'm a good five inches taller than he is. And wider, too.

"Fair is fair," I say in a voice I hope is low and threatening. Tracer goes pale and takes half a step back. I'm starting to like this being an adult thing. Intimidation has its high points.

"Yeah? Well, we'll see about this," he mutters. "A townie getting my survival suit when she can't even use it."

"Yes, she can," Geneva says, coming back on deck, wiping her hands dry on her pant legs. "Barbara here's just joined the crew."

"What!" Tracer shrieks. "*Her! She* can't replace Monroe! Nobody can!"

"I—I'm not trying to replace anyone," I stammer. I don't know a thing about Monroe, but I know no other dog will ever be Santa Barbara. And no other woman my dad hooks up with could ever replace my mom. It's probably the same way with friends. Suddenly intimidating Tracer doesn't seem like fun anymore.

"Don't get your panties in a bunch," Geneva says to Tracer, and pats him on the shoulder. "She's not replacing anybody. Just helping out with the pots when we need it. Look at it this way." She drops her voice to a stage whisper. "If things don't work out with her, maybe you'll get to keep the survival suit anyway." It takes me a second to realize "not working out" up here means dying, like Monroe. I go pale, but Geneva winks at me to tell me she's joking. Tracer gets even madder.

"Where's Harley? This isn't over yet," he says, and he storms off to the wheelhouse to lodge his complaint.

"Well, that's gonna take a while," Geneva says to me with a smile. "Let's hold off on the boat tour. How about we do that shopping trip now? Radio says the Fish and Game Department's opening the season tomorrow. We've got to be ready."

I hoist my bag onto my back again for the walk into town.

Kodiak is a knot of little streets once you get off the main drag along the harbor. And every square inch of sidewalk is packed with crabbers running last-minute errands like us. I follow Geneva, who seems to have some sort of inner compass, like a bird flying south for the winter. The hills we climb are steeper than the ones in Sitka, and soon I wish I'd left my backpack on the *Miranda Lee*.

"Hey, Geneva," a big bear of a man says with a wave as we brush by.

"Hey, Paulie," Geneva waves back. "How's Edna?" She repeats the exchange with what seems like every fifth person on the busy little streets.

"Hey, Charlie, this is Barb. Our new crewmate."

People tip their caps or nod at me, but not before they give me a long once-over, taking in my height, squinting at my too-young face. I decide not to add to the likelihood of being caught by speaking and tripping myself up. So I just nod back and try to look even taller.

It seems to work. No one questions me.

"They like you," Geneva tells me. "They heard you whipped Tracer's butt at the Polar Bar. That's almost as good as saving a life out here."

I can't help smiling. It seems grown-ups are just as bad as kids when it comes to bullies—they like to see the big kids get beat up too.

"Here we are," Geneva says at last, and we duck into a big, low storefront that seems to serve two purposes—post office and marine outfitter.

"Go on, pick out a sleeping bag and a first-aid kit for your bunk. Then we'll see if we can find a pair of bib pants and gloves that suit you."

"Okay." I wave and head off down the crowded aisles. A few of these shoppers might even be the same people I flew up here with. I find the sleeping bags and check the price tag. My heart sinks to the floor. I've got twenty dollars and a maxed-out credit card in my pocket. Without more money, my adulthood is going to be pretty short-lived. I find Geneva by the long underwear.

"Geneva?" She turns around, holding a pair of gray thermal pants up to her waist for sizing.

"Yeah, hon? Finding what you want?"

"Well, not exactly. I . . . uh . . . can't . . ." For some reason it's hard to say. I've never thought of myself as proud. I just try not to look helpless. But right now that's exactly what I am. Suck it up, Lucy girl. Just say it.

"I'm, uh, kind of broke. I can't afford this stuff."

Geneva's face softens with sympathy. "Of course not, honey. Nobody can, first time around. I should've told you not to worry. Harley runs a tab for us. It'll come out of your first paycheck. Everybody comes up here on a budget."

Hallelujah. I breathe a sigh of relief. "Okay. Good. Thanks."

"All part of the deal, Barb. Just be glad you won that survival suit. That would jack up the price more than you want to know. That's why Tracer wants it so bad. Too cheap to pony up on his own. Now let's pick out some boots and gloves."

By the time we reach the counter, I'm loaded down with more stuff than I think I've owned in my life. I dump my new sleeping bag, first-aid kit, insulated socks, waterproof boots, and bright yellow bib pants on the counter, along with a stash of candy bars and salmon jerky and who knows what else. I don't even want to see how much it's all going to cost. Geneva handles the transaction.

"How ya doin', Henry?" Geneva says to the guy behind the counter, a little man with a wispy gray mustache.

"Not so bad, yourself?"

"Brilliant, as always," she tells him. "Henry, I'd like you to meet Barb, the newest member of our crew."

"Pleased to meet you, Barb," he says, and extends a hand. I shake it as firmly as I can, and he seems satisfied when he finally lets go.

"Good grip you got there, ma'am. You'll do good on the *Miranda Lee*."

"Told you so." Geneva grins at me with a wink.

Henry rings up the tab. I wince in spite of myself. It's comfortably into the hundreds. The high hundreds. My first day as an adult and I might as well be an indentured servant. Now this crabbing thing *has* to work out.

"Geneva, you don't have to keep introducing me to people," I tell her as we slip back into the main stream of foot traffic. I want to be noticed as little as possible. If anyone guesses my age before I pay off that tab, I'm in big trouble.

"Honey, what are you talking about? You're a celebrity. Look at these faces around you. They already know about you from the bar last night. I'm just telling them your name. Best way to make friends. And everybody needs those, right?"

Right. Of course she's right. No one here has a clue who I am. I'm not the oversized kid of a drunk. I'm just me. Well, I'm Barb, technically, but that's me all the same. It's weird to have strangers smile at me with admiration. That's new. But that's the point, Lucy girl—a new life.

The next person Geneva introduces me to I decide to be friendlier to. This time around, it's an older man named Cap'n George. He looks like the classic fisherman: bristling gray beard, leathery skin, and a pipe clamped between his teeth.

"Own part of most of the processing plants out in the bay," he explains to me by way of introduction. I nod and try to look suitably impressed, but honestly it doesn't mean much to me.

Geneva can tell, I guess, because she says, "This man's got a bigger share of the industry in Kodiak than most other men combined."

Cap'n George grins a toothy smile and starts to whistle his way down the street. Two seconds later a big black wolf of a dog comes loping up. Without hesitating, he comes right up to me and sniffs my hand.

"This is Killit. He'll be a good friend if you treat him right."

"Hey, Killit," I say, and kneel to scratch him on the chest. Killit has a dangerous look in his eyes, but it melts when the scratching gets good. It makes me think of Bar, and for a minute I can't look back up at the humans.

"This woman knows a thing or two about dogs," George says with a nudge to Geneva.

"She knows a good one when she sees one," Geneva replies. "Come on, Barbara, time to get that nickel tour."

"Bye, Cap'n George." I wave. Of all the people I've met in Kodiak, I think I like him best. If a dog like Killit thinks he's worthwhile, then he must be.

But being with Killit has made me miss Bar. I fall silent for the rest of the trip back to the *Miranda Lee*.

Tracer is on deck when we arrive. He turns his back and ignores me when I come on board.

"A little help here," Geneva says to him in a way that makes me realize she's somehow his superior here on the boat. Tracer takes our bags without a word, but he gives me a dirty look as he brushes by.

"Ignore him," Geneva advises me. "I'll show you where you'll bunk."

The *Miranda Lee*'s bigger than it looks from the outside, but that's not saying much. Whoever built her packed a whole bunch of rooms into a tiny space, but it works. The cabin houses two rooms behind the wheelhouse, with a door that lets out onto the back deck. The wheelhouse also has doors at the front, or foredeck, of the boat. Geneva takes me through the back door of the cabin into the galley, a tiny kitchen with a table and a couple of benches bolted to the floor.

"What's the chalk for?" I ask, pointing at the fat white line drawn around the front of the stove.

"That's the fault line," Geneva says. "If you cross it and get in the way while I'm cooking, what happens to you next is your own damn fault." She smiles and shakes her head. "Ask Tracer, he'll tell you." I smile back and make a mental note to watch my step in the galley.

"Head's down the hall here." Geneva points to a bathroom with a sliding door. "And here's where the beds are." Everybody doesn't sleep at once on board, I guess. The bunkroom only holds four cots. "Door at the end of the hall goes to the wheelhouse."

Geneva climbs down a ladder set along the hallway. "There's storage down here in the hull, and a few closets." I follow her down into the hold.

"Your survival suit's in one of these," Geneva says, pointing with her chin toward a row of doors.

She opens each closet, stowing supplies. Eventually she opens the closet that holds the infamous survival suit. I take an involuntary step back. "It's . . ."

". . . big," Geneva finishes for me. It is big. In fact, it's more than big. It looks like a giant yellow body hanging in a freezer. Now I'm starting to understand what a survival suit is for.

"Don't fold these things or you could cause a leak. Seals you in, two sweaters, parka, and all. Keeps you afloat for as long as it takes to save you. But it won't keep you warm all that long." Geneva displays the suit with a shrug. "Still, it's brand new, never been used. Nicer than most, and a heck of a lot better than nothing."

I reach out to touch my new prize. It's a tough, rubbery material, like a cross between a ski glove and a diving suit.

"Do you have a suit too?"

Geneva shakes her head. "Too expensive. Monroe had a good poker night and won this on the last hand. Forgot all about it when the storm hit. One thing about a suit. It can't help you if you don't let it.

"Well, that's my two cents. Consider it a refund on your tour." She points the way back up the ladder.

"Shall we? Coffeepot's always on in the galley and in the wheelhouse. Harley likes to keep it going when we get into a real run."

"Where is Harley?" Something about him makes me nervous. I'll need to be on my toes around him, I know.

"Oh, he's around somewhere. Don't worry. You're part of the crew now. He'll treat you with the same disregard he treats all of us with." She smiles. "He's a puzzle, that one. But a good man."

I decide I'll have to take her word for it as we head back up the ladder to the wheelhouse.

She pushes through the door. The wheelhouse has windows halfway up to the ceiling. The rest is all battered electronic equipment. "Radio, depth finder, and radar so we can find our pots." Geneva points to each black box, but they all look the same to me. She turns around and indicates the wide area along the back wall. "More than likely, this is where we'll all be sleeping when the crabbing is hot. Four hours down, then back to it. Think you're up to it?"

I nod, but I have no idea if I am or not. I've done quite a bit on less sleep. But something tells me going to high school isn't exactly the same as the kind of hard labor they do out here.

"Sure," I finally say, just to make myself feel better. And I do feel better, because I've got a roof of sorts over my head and a new friend in Geneva—and I'm a hero in a small town I've never been to before. Lucy the Adult is shaping up pretty nicely.

"That's about it," Geneva announces as we loop back out onto the deck.

"Got the nickel tour, I see," Don calls to us from the stern. "Make sure you get some change back." He winks at me. "Not much, but she's a good boat. Kept us well for a long time, wouldn't you say?"

Geneva smiles at me. "Barbara, you'll do just fine here."

"Hey, folks," Harley calls, coming up the pier in his oilskins. "Season opens tomorrow for sure. We're heading out."

Clattering noises ring out all over the *Miranda Lee* as Don stows his tools and Tracer comes down from the rigging. "Yeeeeeehaaaaww!" Don whoops to the sky. "Bering Sea, here we come!"

And me, I'm not nervous. Not one bit.

CHAPTER 6

February 3

BERING SEA, ALASKA

The Bering Sea is not at all what I imagined. It's beautiful. Prettier than heaven, if that's possible. There are towers of ice rising out of the water—polar caps, I know, but that always sounds like a hat for a polar bear and can't compare to what it really means. Out on deck alone for the first time, I feel small next to the ocean and the sky. Like there's room for giants in the world after all.

It's four-thirty in the morning. We're all sitting at the edge of the bay in Kodiak waiting for the Fish and Game folks to fire the gun signaling the start of the season. I've never seen so many boats lined up, like kids in a potato-sack race.

It's pitch-black up here until almost nine o'clock in the morning this time of year, and usually it's so rainy there's no sign of moon or stars. But this morning we have one of those clear, gorgeous skies where you can see every star ever made in heaven. Even the ice floes seem to glow long after the moon goes down.

Geneva makes omelets for everyone—light and fluffy, full of the sweet smoked salmon she bought back in town yesterday. We eat, and sit and wait. Tracer keeps giving me dirty looks. I have to admit, I don't particularly like my new prize, but I'd never give him the satisfaction of knowing it. Adults aren't supposed to back down, so I won't. Monroe's survival suit is mine, fair and square.

"Barbara, let me show you something." Don interrupts my thoughts. He grabs his parka and leads me out on deck to the crab traps. "See that bucket inside there?" It looks like a wire basket inside the bigger basket of the cage. "That's the bait bucket. When we get out a little further, Geneva'll show you how to fill it with herring. Then we'll drop the pots with these winches." He points to the pulley system on the side masts. "Harley lets them soak a few days underwater to give the crabs a chance to get inside. Then we come back and pull 'em out again.

"Whatever we keep goes down here." He lifts a trap door set in the middle of the back deck. It opens into a deep well punched full of holes. "Those holes let the seawater in. Best way to keep the crabs kicking until we get back to shore." He shuts the lid again.

"Just wanted to give you a heads-up before it gets going. Once the crab's on and we start pulling, we hardly ever stop.

"Pay attention out there," he adds. "These old jars are big and dangerous when the sea is high. You've got to watch your own back all the time."

"Thanks, Don." My mind goes back over everything he's shown me. One last cram session before the final, Lucy. This isn't a test I can afford to fail. We lean against the rail and watch the waves. A light drizzle is falling, but it is still beautiful out here. I shove my hands in my pockets. "Don? How long have you been doing this?"

"Crabbing? Shoot, I don't know. Since I was a kid . . . nineteen, twenty maybe? Younger than you are now."

"Wow. That is young." I want to laugh, but Don couldn't possibly guess the joke.

"Not that I'm over the hill yet," he continues. "Got at least fifty years of work left in me. Especially if Harley's got anything to say about it." He laughs and leads the way inside.

Since I'm preparing for the work ahead, I decide to go below to examine my survival suit. It's a big, ugly thing. Just my size, I'd guess. I start to try it on, just to make sure—knowing we're heading out today makes me want to be prepared—but it gives me the creeps to try on something that belonged to a dead man. And it didn't do him any good, so maybe it's jinxed. But then again, it didn't help Monroe because he never even got it on.

Finally, by six o'clock, the Fish and Game guys have counted enough crab in the area. The Coast Guard sends up a signal flare and all the radios squawk to life. Harley guns the motor. Don yells, "Yeehaw!" and we take off.

We stay at top speed all morning. Geneva says we'll reach our first spot by tonight. That's when the work really begins. For now I'm just sitting and watching the landscape as it goes from Kodiak gray-white to tundra blue-white in nothing flat. Eventually there's only water as far as the eye can see. A far cry from my little bedroom back home.

I can hear Tracer up at the wheelhouse still arguing with Harley over the survival suit, so when Geneva and Don tromp up the deck past me, I join them to get away.

Don's got a knotted-up old rag or something in his mouth and he's chewing on it like it's beef jerky.

"Will you stop chewing that nasty thing?" Geneva wrinkles her face in disgust.

"I chew my rag to calm my nerves," Don says.

"And it cleans my teeth. It's either this or you give me back my tobacco."

"Absolutely not," Geneva tells him. "Fish guts are bad enough without having to watch you hawk spit into them."

"Well, Barb don't mind my chewin', do ya, Barb?"

I don't want to get caught in the middle of even a silly disagreement my second day out, so I just blink at him and look away. Stay low and stay out of the way.

"See!" exclaims Don, like I just helped him win the argument. Geneva waves him off.

"Don, I don't care if *God* says it's okay, you can't go chewing that rot on this boat!"

"If you wasn't a woman, I'd . . ." Don trails off before he completes the threat. Instead of throwing a drunken punch like some of my dad's pals might have, he simply sits down beside me and changes the subject.

"One time we were out here, and about the only thing keeping me alive was knowing there was a cigarette waiting for me at the end of the shift. But back then, Geneva hated the smoke. *She's* the one who got me on chaw to begin with. Thought it'd keep me on deck and I'd work harder without all that secondhand smoke crap she's worried about. Well, look at her now. Nag, nag, nag. She can't tell me what to do."

I nod. I know how he feels. But I also notice that he puts the rag away and finds a partially frozen stick of gum to chew instead.

"You're all right, Barb. You don't nag like most women do." I want to say it's because I'm not a woman. But I just shrug and try not to smile when he gets the gum caught in his beard.

Our first crabbing spot looks like every other piece of water out here on the Bering—dark and choppy. A bank of rain clouds rolls in, tossing down a little snow for good measure. With the exception of an occasional blink of light from other crab boats, there's not much to distinguish this spot from any other we've passed. Still, Harley says this is it, so I pretend not to be tired, drag my new bib pants on over my rubber boots, and head out onto the deck.

The deck is slick with ice. I have to crouch down to keep my balance. Geneva shows me around the crab pots—big suckers, about eight hundred pounds each. Fifteen of them we have to bait and lower into the water by motorized winch and drop to the bottom of the ocean. "Watch," she says, "then work."

I stand back against the wall of the wheelhouse and watch the crew of the *Miranda Lee* do their thing.

Don and Tracer take turns whacking at the bait—frozen herring, Don says—with a sledgehammer, breaking the fish into bits. Once they're done, Geneva steps in, shoveling bait into a basket inside the trap.

"Reach me that hook up there," she says, motioning to me. The hook dangles a few feet over her head from a line on one of the side masts. I grab it easily and pass it to her, feeding down the line until she's got enough slack to hook it to the first pot.

"I knew you'd be a natural fit," she says with a grin.

I can't help grinning too as I watch her latch the hook to the top of the first pot. Lucy the Giant, a natural fit. A natural *anything*. Who'd've thought it?

"Here we go," Don shouts, and the crane hoists the first pot into the sea. The line whizzes by and suddenly stops as the pot hits bottom. Tracer attaches the end of the line to a buoy that he drops overboard, the only sign of where the pot has gone.

"And that's how it's done." Geneva winks. There's no time to ask questions. Harley's got us on a schedule, and there are fourteen more pots to go.

Despite my fears about hard labor, the work is actually pretty light. Geneva shows me the quickest way to bait the traps with big chunks of cod and herring, like shoveling coal, and how to hook the pots, or jars as they sometimes call them, to the pulleys for hoisting. I help where I can by reaching places for her that

I guess only Monroe was tall enough to reach before. With the way the waves toss the boat around, climbing on top of the pots to reach the hooks would probably be a bad idea.

Tracer and Don set the traps, using a motorized winch to heave them off the deck and into the water. Each trap has a line that Tracer attaches to another floating buoy. Markings identify the buoys and the traps as ours. "That way they're easier to find on the way back around," Don explains.

Tracer snorts, "Greenhorn," and shakes his head. I pretend not to hear him.

We drop three traps at the first spot; then Harley hauls anchor and moves the boat a little ways before we drop a few more. When I can't help, I just step aside and try to stay out of the way. For the first hour I can feel Harley watching me. He makes me nervous. What's worse, the colder it gets, the more rubbery my fingers feel. The hooks start slipping between them like little fish, and I keep dropping the bait.

"Don't let him shake you," Don whispers to me, wiping the rain from his mustache. "He's just watching out for you. Had enough bad luck for one year. He won't let any of us get careless out here."

"Okay," I say, but I still feel jumpy. Harley's barely said three words to me since we set sail.

We bait and drop and bait and drop until my arms are as rubbery as my fingers. The wind and rain build until I almost can't feel them as anything but a faint drumming on my frozen face. Only the icy waves, slapping over the rails to hit us in the face, keep me from going completely numb. So this is crabbing, I think. Way to go, Lucy girl.

When all the traps are finally set, I'm shocked to look at my watch and discover we've worked through the night and all of the next day. The rain has been coming down so hard I never noticed the sunrise or sunset. Harley swings the *Miranda Lee* back around so we can start picking them up again.

"Well, gang. We've gotta let the pots soak," Harley announces over coffee. We seem to drink coffee any time of day here. It's better than McDonald's finest, and more importantly, it's always hot. I've never been so cold in my life. The galley feels like an oven after being on deck. I wrap my hands around my mug to get the feeling back in them.

"It looks like we've got a bit of a storm brewing. Nothing we can't ride out. Rest while you can."

Everybody else stays put, but Geneva and Don exchange a look. Don turns to me.

"Why don't you grab some sleep?" Don says. I must admit I'm feeling kind of ragged around the edges, so I don't argue. It wouldn't do to have me falling asleep on deck in the middle of work. I head back to the bunkroom, but I can't sleep. My head won't let me.

It's been four days since I left Sitka. Now that we've set sail, I'm pretty much here for the season—four weeks, Geneva tells me, or until our crab tank is full. Not that I want to go back. Bar is gone. I've got nothing left there now but my dad, my little room, and all the reasons I left in the first place.

I turn onto my stomach and bury my face in my pillow. Who will Murph call to bring my dad home when he's too far gone to drive, I wonder? Who will pull Sheila out of the next locker? My stomach churns. For a minute I think I will be seasick after all.

Get a grip, Lucy girl. It's only been four days. If the world had ended, somehow I would know.

Four days. Crap. The math clicks into place. Bar's ashes will be showing up at my house tomorrow or the next day. If my dad's home at all, it's more than likely he'll just toss her out with the rest of the cans. Bar deserves better than that. I should have called the doctor's office and asked them to hold her for me. Or if I'd just told Sheila what was going on, she could have kept them for me. Of course, if I'd just told Sheila about Bar in the first place, maybe she could have helped. Maybe Bar would still be alive today.

Another wave of nausea hits me and I close my eyes tight. Maybe keeping secrets costs too much. But secrets are all I have left. If I just keep to myself, things will turn out okay. They have to.

—/—

I must've dozed off, because the next thing I know it's three A.M. Tracer's boot is my alarm clock. "Stop hogging the bunk," he complains. "Harley wants you up on anchor watch."

"What's that?" I'm foggy, but I'm up in an instant. If Harley's asking, I better learn quick.

"Anchor watch," Tracer says, rolling his eyes. Like any idiot in the world would know what he's talking about. "Crew's asleep, 'cept for Harley, and he's in the wheelhouse. Somebody's gotta get outside and keep an eye on the anchor."

I pull on my coat and gloves. Geneva and Don are dead asleep in the other bunks. "Okay," I mumble, and head out on deck.

The anchor is off the starboard bow. I don't know the best place to watch it from, but higher seems better. So I climb the wheelhouse like I've seen Tracer do so many times and sit on his perch, watching the anchor chain where it disappears into the icy water.

Cold doesn't begin to describe how I feel. My nose hairs are crackling. I pull my hat around my ears and try to keep warm.

I should never have signed on for this. It was giddiness, Lucy. Too much oxygen out here on the ocean. Or just sheer exhaustion. Yep, that's what it was. Sheer exhaustion. Whatever made me think crabbing was the life for me was crazy. This is no kind of life for anyone.

I've got blisters. On my hands and my lips. Not from heat of course, but from the cold. It turns out the cold can burn right through the lining in your gloves, especially if you don't keep the insides dry. Getting them wet was my mistake, sure, and I'm paying for it. But Tracer won't let me live it down. Geneva is better. She helped me put some salve on them. They don't hurt so much now. Harley says I can still work. And I guess I have to. I owe him a lot of money right now.

Lucy girl, what have you gotten yourself into? I try not to think about it. Instead, I take a deep breath and look around.

It's beautiful out here tonight, in an eerie way. The clouds are low, and the waves rise up to meet them like stalagmites in a cave. Tonight I'm not the outsider, the whole boat is.

"Barbara!"

"Yessir!" I almost fall off my perch. Harley's glaring at me from the door of the wheelhouse.

"What the hell are you doing up there?"

"Uh, anchor watch, sir. Sorry . . . I was just looking around. I'll, I'll d-do b-better." The cold is making me stutter, and I sound worse by the minute. Great, Luce. Way to make a good impression.

"Anchor watch?" Harley snorts. "Tracer put you up to this?"

"Yessir. Said you needed me out here. I thought up here'd give me the best view."

"We've got a storm coming on. Up there'll give you pneumonia and that's about it." He shakes his head. "Get inside, Barbara. Tracer's just yanking your chain."

Cold as I am, I can feel my face grow hot. Damn it, Lucy. You'll fall for anything. If this doesn't give me away, nothing will.

But it doesn't give me away. "Relax. Everybody gets it in the beginning," Harley explains as I try to warm up over a cup of tea in the galley. "Don did it to Geneva, and they both did it to Tracer. It's usually worse if you're a woman. You'll get the hang of it." He doesn't stick around for more small talk. Just pours a cup of coffee and heads back to the wheelhouse.

When the feeling comes back to my fingers, I head below and fall fast asleep.

—/—

It feels like I've been asleep only a minute when I hear, "All hands—we've got ice! Ice!" That's the kind of news that would keep one of my dad's drinking parties going all night. I sit up groggily and look out the portal. Suddenly I understand what it means to have ice in the Bering Sea.

Sheets of it. Coating the lines like wax on candlewicks. But this is inches thick. And with each new wave, another half-inch is forming on everything. The *Miranda Lee* groans under the weight, and she starts to list to the left. I realize if we lean over any farther, we're going to flip over and go under.

In nothing flat I'm dressed and sliding into Monroe's survival suit. It still gives me the creeps, but better safe than sorry. If I go under, I can't expect anyone to jump in and save me.

The suit is a little too big in some places, but I know I'll be glad of the extra warmth it traps. Grabbing my work gloves, I head topside.

"What can I do?" I ask. Harley glances at my survival suit. I can only guess he's thinking of Monroe. But maybe not, because he's already pointing at the windows. They're encased in a sheet of ice, with little more than a handprint-sized clearing for us to see through.

"Break the ice off the windows," he tells me, shouting to be heard above the sound of the others, already on deck swinging sledgehammers to clear the pots before they get too heavy and sink us all. Sleet is coming out of the sky in sheets, and the waves are pounding over the rails of the aft deck. The crab pots have frozen into glaciers of groaning ice and metal. The crew looks tiny against the storm.

"I can't steer us out of here if I can't see," Harley shouts. "Clear the windows, then help the others. Keep the pots clear."

Hammer in hand, I head outside, wondering how I can break the ice without shattering the glass right along with it.

After a few timid strikes and a wind-carried curse from Geneva, I start whaling on the glass like there's no tomorrow. Because I realize there might not be a tomorrow and I'm stupid for even being here. At least I had a chance of surviving in Sitka. Even with the booze and the fighting and everything else, at least I had a damn chance. Here, nobody gives a crap whether I live or die. And I willingly picked *this* over home?

I swing with the full force of my oversized body and hear something shatter—ice, thank God; not glass, but ice, three inches of it, spiderwebbing and shattering all over the place. Through the window I see Harley give me a thumbs-up and point to the other windows. Four more panels to go, and the sleet is already caking up again on the one I just cleared.

My fingers are numb, my toes nonexistent. Waves batter us and I get tossed first into the railing, then the wheelhouse, and then a body—Tracer. We brace our backs up against each other—he's clearing the pots, I'm still working on the wheelhouse windows.

Tracer screams above the wind. I'm swinging too hard to hear him, and I guess I'm in his way, because his screams get louder. "*Back off!*" I clear my window; then I move, and I can only think that my dad's stinking beer breath would be better than this bitter cold, this ungrateful, unyielding ice, and this bastard yelling at my back, making me feel like I'm to blame, like none of this would've happened if I hadn't come on board and tried to take a dead man's place.

"Damn it, Tracer, watch those pots!" Harley's voice comes, a sharp bark from the wheelhouse.

Tracer just keeps cursing, and it's not until Don and Geneva join in that I realize it's not me he's mad at. It's the weather. It's nature. It's God. And he keeps cursing—they all do. They swear against their mothers, their fathers, all things they consider holy. Geneva's grimacing against the strain and Tracer's laughing and Don's screaming as he breaks the ice on the pots. But the ice keeps building up again and again. I finally clear the windows and join the others at the pots. We swing and swing and it's starting to work even though my shoulders are aching. If I'm going to die here, I'm going to die doing something about it. I'm not wasting away like my dad, or quitting like my mother. I'm not giving up. I'll keep going until I don't have any more left in me.

And maybe the wind is dying just a little, and maybe the snow isn't falling so fast and the waves aren't crashing so high, because I stop, just for an instant. I stop and I look up. Don is beside me now, looking me dead in the eye. He keeps swinging at the pots, but when he looks at me, his face goes even whiter than the snow and ice covering his beard.

A scream like nothing I've ever heard shatters my eardrums. A ton of crab pot slides faster than we can move. The pot slams Don against the wheelhouse, crushing his thigh like a walnut.

"Out of the way, Barb!" Geneva screams at me. She shoves past me out of nowhere, and Harley is out on deck and I'm useless as they heave and heave and heave, dragging back the killing pot. Finally I understand and I join them. The wind is dying and so is Don. Dying on the deck of the *Miranda Lee,* his leg turned to jelly, held together by his bib pants and his survival suit.

Oh, no, I think. Oh God, no. This is the way it happens, this is the way it ends. "Oh God, Don!" I shout, but I'm really whispering, and I know because I can hear Harley saying, "Barb, keep breaking that ice. Now, damn it!"

And I move, and I break. I break like the ice that shatters beneath my numb hands. Hands that shake and quiver with the dull thuds that go straight to my heart, straight to my brain. And I think about *The Old Man and the Sea.* I think about Santiago eating sweet dolphin fish as his hands grow raw holding the line. And Bar being wheeled away into that back room, alone with strangers. And I swing, and I shatter, and I ache.

When the storm finally passes, it's like the calm after my dad's gone on one of his really big binges, when I want to stay quiet so I don't bring back any of the memories of what happened in the night. But I can't because my mind is on fire.

There's blood frozen to the deck. Harley sits next to Don's bunk, one hand holding a cup of coffee, the other holding Don's hand. The cot isn't big enough for Don to lie down on. I'm glad when the Coast Guard finally shows up in their big white rescue boat to take him back to Kodiak and the hospital, where he'll sit out the rest of the season.

"He'll live," the Coast Guard medic says to me. His eyes are warm and brown. The warmest thing I've seen since last night. My own face must look ghastly, because he shakes his head and says, "Getting younger every year."

A chill runs down my spine. Just when I thought I couldn't get any colder. For a split second I think he knows. I think he's on to me. He knows I'm only fifteen and knee-deep in the scariest crap I've ever seen. And just for that split second, I *want* him to know. I want to cry like a fifteen-year-old, cry and have him hold me and tell me it'll be all right and take me away.

But he doesn't. Instead, the medic treats me like a crabber, weathered, someone who's seen it all. He gives me a slap on the back, like he's been too sensitive already. "Weather's turned," he says. "Not another storm like that due in for a few days, I suspect."

I nod stiffly and rub the back of my neck. "Good fishing," he says, and salutes me with a nod before maneuvering the plank joining our boats together.

"You'll get your share, Don," Harley says as they lift his gurney up over the railing. "Like you worked the full time. Don't you worry." Don nods gratefully and closes his eyes against the pain.

I hang my head because I want to say something, but I can't think of anything worthwhile. Tracer glares at me from behind the newly cleared pots. Suddenly I feel far, far from home.

Tears well up from deep inside me and start rolling down my face before I can stop them.

Geneva shows up beside me. "Don't cry, girl," she tells me. "The wind'll freeze the tears to your face. You'll get burn marks on your cheeks."

It's so ridiculous I almost laugh. It never got this cold in Sitka. But I never let anyone see me cry in Sitka either. So when Harley says, "That's the crab-bing life," I imitate his shrug and shuffle to the stern of the boat, where the wheelhouse will hide me, and I watch the Coast Guard carry Don off. Don, who said he liked me. Don, who tried to make me feel like I belonged. And I wonder if he'd treat me the same if he knew I was just fifteen, and far weaker than my body had a right to be.

I sit there for a long time, feeling the engine chug as Harley points the *Miranda Lee* once again toward our crab pots. I peel off my work gloves and wipe my nose on the cotton undergloves, and I search the waves for orcas that never come.

And I cry. Damn the windburn, I cry. The Bering Sea isn't Sitka. There is no shame in what I feel. When I finally get up, I don't know if the tears have burned me or if that was just a wives' tale. But I don't care. I am still alive. I don't care who sees my scars.

CHAPTER 7

February 6

BERING SEA, ALASKA

I am in over my head. The Coast Guard took Don away over three hours ago, and we are all stuck here, feeling dead in the water. Except Harley. Harley is like a demon, cracking a whip over the *Miranda Lee*, driving us back to the crab pots. We've lost precious time because of the storm, and there's plenty riding on our success with a good catch. We'll need to pull pots night and day now. With Don gone, I'm going to have to help carry his load.

But I don't think I can do it.

I thought life was hard in Sitka. I thought it was about my dad, about me getting the short end of the stick as a kid. But there are bigger things to worry about out here at sea. Life-and-death things fifteen-year-olds don't usually face. Even fifteen-year-olds as big as me. I'm scared.

"Look alive, people!" Harley yells. We're back at the first set of pots and the look on Harley's face says it's the most important spot of all. It's the spot where we turn our luck around.

My fingers feel stiff as I pull my work gloves on. I can't tell if it's from the cold or just lack of will.

"Tuck your pants with these, Barb, or you'll get soaked," Geneva says, with a nod toward my feet. She hands me a pair of thick rubber bands. This is my first time really doing the work part of crabbing. I should take her advice, but I can't seem to make myself care.

Geneva shrugs. It's not until Tracer starts laughing that I bend to do as she says. I get one pant leg strapped down when a wave dashes overboard, filling my other boot like a cup.

"Crap," I mutter.

Tracer bursts into a whoop of laughter, and Geneva gives me a sympathetic smile. My toes are starting to freeze, thanks to the ice-water bath. "Get inside and get some new socks on before you get frostbite," she tells me. I run and do as she says. By the time I get back, my toes are warm but Harley's frowning at me. The first buoy is already alongside us.

Geneva grabs the buoy with a hook and signals Tracer to start the crane. I rush to help Geneva haul the line hand over hand to hoist the first of the traps on deck. She expertly coils the line as it races through our hands. I make a mess of it, but she won't let me stop. "Keep it up," she says. "You'll learn."

As the first pot rises from the water, full of squirming purple life, I wonder if this is the trap that crushed Don.

"Stop woolgathering and hit it!" Harley shouts. I snap out of it to see this great big pot swinging up over our heads, wriggling with crabs. We lower it on deck and Tracer and Geneva get to work sorting and picking.

"These are king crabs, Barb," Geneva tells me. She grabs a huge crab from the pot and flips it over. "See the way the shell forms that skinny point on the belly here? That means it's a male. It's only legal to keep males this size. Everything else goes back in the water. Females get to breed, and the small males get a chance to grow."

The first crab I grab must weigh at least eight pounds. I struggle to grip it and jab my finger on one of its barbed legs.

"Crap!" I drop it and shake my hand. Luckily my work gloves save me from any real damage. Tracer smirks. Harley gives me a hard look, then grabs a crab himself—by the body, not the legs. Apparently king crabs don't have thorny butts.

I reach down, wrap my gloves around my crab from behind, and heave it, double-handed, into the well. My one crab hits the water with a pathetic splash.

Tracer shakes his head, but Geneva smiles. She tosses crabs in rapid-fire motion and I try to keep pace.

Once I get the hang of how to avoid the barbs, it's just yank and toss, yank and toss, yank and toss. You forget everything but the weight of the crab in your hands, judging how hard to throw it to reach the well. It's like being in a dream, all big yellow hands and squirming shells.

It goes like this for hours, days it seems. Empty one pot, rebait and drop it, then haul up another one. I sneak a peek at my watch. It's only been forty-five minutes. Every muscle in my body hurts so much it's forgotten how to just ache. For all my size and supposed strength, I feel used up. But with every new pain in my arms, the rest of me hurts a little less. So I keep hauling and let crabbing numb my mind the way a whole night of walking around Sitka never could.

Harley swings by occasionally with a pot of coffee for everyone. Then he gets right back to helping us sort our catch. With the wind in our faces and the salty ocean smell in the air, I feel like we should be singing a song. Something rowdy and stoic about hauling the harvest from the sea. But I don't know any songs like that, and since no one else is volunteering, I figure it would be a bad idea for me to try to make something up.

At some point Harley taps me on the shoulder and says, "Sleep." My shoulders throb, but I don't even have the energy to wince when he touches me. I blink at him and look around—it's dark. We've been crabbing all day, into the night. Harley whacks me on the back again to get my attention. He waves a gloved hand in my face, the thumb curled in. "Four, and counting," he says, and drifts off down the deck. Four hours of sleep. It won't be enough.

Now I know why we don't sleep below decks when we're working. I barely make it to the wheelhouse before I collapse. I don't even notice if the deck shudders beneath me when I hit it. I just sink, fast and completely, into sleep. My last conscious thought is, How am I ever going to finish Hemingway?

There's something about being on the water that changes the way you dream. Dreams are bigger, somehow. Santa Barbara is looking at me from the pier. "You're just gonna sit there?" she asks, in a deeper voice than I would ever have consciously imagined for her. Her head tilts to the side in a funny, raised-ear way, like those old *Little Rascals* episodes where the dog, Petey, sees something he doesn't understand.

I can't see myself, but I know I'm offshore and I'm floating in warm, salty water. "That's the idea, Bar," I tell her. She's far away, but we're not shouting. It's like this little dream space is just for her and me.

I look around and see sailboats in their slips, like in the harbor in Sitka. But there's something off about it. Palm trees. Tall, skinny things arching up into the sky. And I realize that this isn't Sitka at all, or even Alaska. This is Santa Barbara, California.

On the dock my dog sighs and shakes her head. "Okay." She shrugs, exasperated. "This can't last forever, though." And she leaps into the water to paddle out to me.

"Why not?" I ask, and I flap my arms in the water. I'm sitting in an inner tube. Nice . . . relaxed. Bar disappears underwater.

"Bar?" I call. No response. I start to panic. "Bar!" I stick my face in the water, eyes stinging with salt, but I can't see her. No bubbles on the surface. And I can't move. The water gets colder. On shore the palm trees are dissolving, changing into what? Pine trees. Sitka pines.

"*SANTA BARBARA . . .*" I yell as loud as I can. My heart pounds. I can't breathe.

And then, *pop!* She hops up out of the water in

front of me, but her grin isn't a dog grin, it's the thousand-toothed grin of an orca, a killer whale.

"Time to grow up!" she yips at me, and her rough tongue licks my face. I yelp and jolt awake.

"Time to get up!" Somebody's shouting at me. I open a bleary eye. Tracer nudges me in the ribs with his boot. "Our shift, our shift, Barb. Get the hell going." My brain seems to flood back into my body in a hot rush. I'm shaking a little as I get my work clothes back in shape, carefully tucking my pant legs into each boot the way I'm supposed to, and head out to the deck in the cold gray dawn. Four hours. I'm bone, dog tired.

Just when I'm about to drift into la-la land again, something briny hits me in the side.

"Ow!" I look up in time to see Geneva grinning at me. A load of slimy green seaweed is sliding down my jacket. Doesn't she ever sleep?

"Hey!" I scoop up another chunk of seaweed and hurl it back at her. I've got a pretty good arm and the seaweed smacks her full in the chest.

"There's more where that came from," she shouts, and from out of nowhere hurls a bucket of water at me.

Half of it hits me, but the other half hits Tracer.

"Damn it!" he hollers, and starts flinging whatever he can find my way—seaweed, shells, little fish, even crabs. I throw them right back, and Geneva joins in, laughing like a little kid.

Suddenly Harley's voice booms from out of the wheelhouse. "That's money you're throwing out there. Earn it or burn it."

Geneva grins, tucking her hair back into her cap. We must both stink like fish now, but who can tell? My nose is too frozen to smell.

"Move it, missy," Geneva says to me, flinging a last little crab at my head. I duck in time and notice the second trap is coming our way.

We set to work again, the same rhythm of pluck and toss, yank and throw, until my arms feel like rubber ropes.

"Look who's getting the hang of it," Harley comments, passing by, checking the lines on traps. I swear he's almost smiling when he says it. And me, I'm grinning ear to ear.

" 'I've been working on the railroad . . . ,' " I sing under my breath, " '. . . all the livelong day!' " It seems to fit the work, so I keep singing it, pausing to grunt or toss a heavy load. " 'I've been working on the . . . rail . . . road . . . just to pass the time awaaaaaaaay.' "

Suddenly Geneva chimes in. " 'Can't you hear the whistle blowing, *rise up early in the morn'!*' "

She winks at me and we both join in on the last

line, " 'Can't you hear the captain shouting: *Dinah, blow your horn!*' "

The cold air feels good slamming into our faces. I could almost dance a jig as we haul the next trap, shouting, " '*Dinah, won't you blow, Dinah, won't you blow, Dinah, won't you blow your hoor-oor-oorn! Dinah, won't you blow, Dinah, won't you blow, Dinah, won't you blow your hhhhhoooooooorrrrn!*' "

I almost fall over when a horn blasts out *Toot Toot!* right on cue. I look up to see Harley grinning at us from the wheelhouse door. "That's what I like to see. The crew that sings together swings together."

"Whatever that means," Geneva hollers back with a grin. But it looks like Harley's right, because even Tracer is tapping his toe, whistling as he works.

"That's about it, gang," Harley says. "Window's up tonight. We're about full up, anyway. We'll hit the processor, then stay out until the next window in a couple of days. Don't stop now, though. I'll tell you when." And he heads back inside to check his instruments or scan the radio or whatever it is he does while we're getting sloppy out here.

"How's it feel, Barb?" Geneva asks me. "Your tour of duty is just about over."

For a minute I forget to be a grown-up. I smile and say, "Awesome."

The processing plant is a big floating barge offshore from Bristol Bay. The crabbers sell their loads here before heading back out for another run. Geneva tells me you can even sleep on board sometimes, and get a meal different from the ones on your boat, if they like you and they've got the room. Over a hundred people, like the college kids I came up here with, work on the processor we tied up to this morning. I can hear them inside, like a hive of bees. Harley clambers past us onto the processor to deal with the plant manager. Tracer and Geneva follow him to talk to old friends on neighboring boats. I find myself left alone, practicing rope coiling.

"Mornin'," a voice says. A man on a scarred old crabbing boat tied a few yards away calls to me across the water. He smiles wide. I nod.

"Good catch?" he asks.

I shrug. Stay low and stay out of the way, Lucy. Things are going well so far. No need to open yourself up to new scrutiny.

"Fair enough." He nods. "Whereabouts you been huntin'?"

His smile gets even wider, more sharklike.

I shrug again and squint up at him. "All looks pretty much the same to me," I say, hoping if I play dumb, he'll leave me alone.

It seems to work. "Fair enough," he says again.

"You must be the one that whipped Tracer at the Polar Bar. Pleased to meetcha." He tips his cap and smiles wider as Geneva climbs back on board.

"Jake," she calls to him. "Are you taking advantage of our newest member here?"

"Not at all, Geneva." He shakes his head. "Just trying to be friendly."

"Yeah, well, be friendly somewhere else." She smiles pleasantly and waits until Jake goes back inside his wheelhouse. Then she turns to me.

"That's Jake Hammond. He's a scoundrel. But from the look on his face, you passed the test."

"What test?" I ask.

"The silence test," she explains. "Rule of the road out here, Lucy. If another crabber asks about your catch and you're dumb enough to tell them, they'll beat you to the best spots next time. Everybody respects a crabber that holds his tongue."

Just then Harley swings back down to the deck of the *Miranda Lee* after conducting negotiations with the plant manager.

"Well," he says with that same hidden smile he gave me earlier, "we didn't do too badly. Frank says he'll wire Don his share." He gives me a look I can't read and says, "I'll pay you out after supper."

Tracer smirks from his usual place beside the traps. Geneva frowns. I have no idea what's going on.

"Now, Harley," she says, "you know we're doing good with all of us here. Why'd you want to change that now?"

Harley makes it all the way to the wheelhouse before he turns around, his cap low over his eyes. "It's not up to me," he says. "Ask her."

Her? "Ask me what?" I say, trying not to sound so befuddled. "What's going on?"

"We're asking you to stay," Geneva says. "When you signed on, you did it for the first run. But it looks like we're going out again in a day or so. Harley never pays us out until we get back to Kodiak. He keeps the money on the books so in case anything happens, the money will still get to our families. Offering to pay you now is his way of offering you the door.

"What do you think?" she asks me with a raised eyebrow, her mouth an expectant little O.

I don't have to think about it. This one thing I know. "I want to stay."

Tracer curses under his breath and kicks some ropes as he stalks away.

"Ignore him." Geneva claps me on the back. "He's just sulking on principle now. Things've just gotten better on the *Miranda Lee,* if you ask me. Maybe she's just been needing a couple of women to steer her right."

I grin at the thought. I'm a woman. Suddenly my

future is stretching before me and I can imagine it, living on the water, part of a crew. Working during the fishing season and doing whatever I want in my downtime. That's what grown-ups get to do. And I think this is what Bar meant in my dream. It's time to grow up. And I just did. I've made it. I really *am* a woman now.

From the wheelhouse Harley tips his cap, then pushes it back some. His eyes sparkle like blue water when he smiles his first real smile and directs it at me. "Welcome aboard," he says. "We're glad to have you."

I smile back. I'm glad too.

CHAPTER 8

February 10

BERING SEA, ALASKA

I love the *Miranda Lee*. It's better than any place I've ever been. Tracer complains that the bunks are too small and he's sick of eating crab every night, but the bunks aren't any smaller than my bed was back home. And crab is better than leftover Big Macs any day. We've been docked in the bay next to the processing plant for the past two days. The next crab fishery—the window of time Fish and Game lets us catch crab—is due to open up tomorrow. Until then we've pretty much got free time. I slept a whole day.

Yesterday Harley set me to work doing little chores around the boat. I've finally gotten the hang of coiling running line, and I'm even learning how to use the crane. All the ropes are coiled, the gears greased, and just about every surface is spit-shined or polished now. She might not be as pretty as the sailboats in Sitka, but the *Miranda Lee* and I get along pretty well.

Harley, I'm discovering, is another story. There is something about him, something familiar. I don't know what it is, but it makes me wish I had more to say to him than *Yessir* or *No, sir*. Maybe it's his way of talking low and still being heard. Like he's never been wrong in his life, never been self-conscious. I wish I was like that.

Sheila wouldn't like him. She'd say he's too gruff or too serious. It's true he smiles just about as often as fish fly, but when he does it's the real thing. And, as much as he scares me, he also makes me feel safe. That's something I haven't felt in a long time.

Outside of giving us chores or updates on the weather, I don't think Harley's said more than twenty words to anyone but Geneva. I mean, I can understand avoiding Tracer—I'm not exactly eloquent around him either. But I'm not sure why he stays away from me. I'm trying not to take it personally. You'd think I'd be used to that sort of thing by now, anyway. I guess I can blame Geneva for being so darn friendly and treating me like a normal person. She's spoiling me.

When the sun rises this morning, we actually see it. The rain clouds have peeled back for a few hours, and it is glorious. Everybody heads outside. Tracer climbs to the top of the wheelhouse with a whittling stick. Harley starts walking laps around the deck, and I drag a chair outside to catch up on *The Old Man and the Sea.*

Now, I know this book is supposed to be a classic, but it's taking more than a hundred pages to catch one fish. So instead of actually reading, I'm hiding behind the pages and sneaking peeks at Harley.

"Morning, Barbara."

"Uh . . . hey. I mean, good morning . . . Harley." He nods and keeps walking laps around the wheelhouse.

I bury myself back in my book.

"Hey, hon." Geneva drags another chair out and joins me. She passes me a mug of coffee, balancing her own cup in the same hand.

"Thanks." I take the mug gratefully. Even at eleven-thirty, the sun's not high enough to cut the cold.

"Don't mind Harley. He's not what we call social. Not anymore, at least."

"What do you mean?"

"Ah, you know the type. He's a good man, but he can't handle his drinking. And drinking used to be the only way he could unwind. That's dangerous, especially in this line of work."

"Is that why he wouldn't drink with you at Monroe's wake?"

Geneva nods. "Partly that. And partly because he couldn't stand Monroe. But he needed him. Not that many people wanted to work on the *Miranda Lee* this year, until Harley proved himself. He didn't crawl out of the bottle more than a couple of years ago, and it's next to impossible for a drunk skipper to regain trust."

She blows on her coffee and smiles.

"No offense, hon, but that's what helped you get the job here. When Monroe died, it made Harley look bad, even though I can swear to you it wasn't his fault. Accidents happen. But Harley has a track record for being . . . less than reliable when he's been drinking. And that can hurt a man pretty bad."

I hang my face over the cloud of steam rising from my cup. I can't imagine Harley as a drunk, or as a danger to his crew. "So he's clean now?"

"Dry as a bone. I've known that man for five years now, seen him drunk and sober. He's straight as an arrow, I can tell you. Won't go near anything that even looks like a bottle these days. Trouble is, if you fish in Kodiak, you can't avoid the bars." She waves her mug in the air, almost spilling her coffee. "Hell, half our business happens over bottles and Beer Nuts. Harley won't do anything to risk his reputation again. Another slipup and they could pull his license. So he mostly avoids the bars. And he avoids the people." She gives me a pointed look.

"The people?" I repeat. Then I realize what she means. Bar people. Drinkers. And to him, that's me. "You mean Harley won't talk to me because of that stupid contest with Tracer?"

Geneva grins at the memory. "Well, I wouldn't call it stupid, but yes, Barb. You can pack it away. And to him that's just an open invitation down the wrong road."

"But that's ridiculous!" I laugh. "I don't drink. I'm not a drinker! I only did that because I—"

"Because you were hurting." Geneva looks at me with those fairy godmother eyes and smiles sadly. "I know, hon. I could tell. But that's the way it always starts, with hurting. Just ask Harley. If you can get him to slow down his pacing."

She pats my leg and rises from her chair just as Harley completes his latest lap.

"Morning, Geneva."

"Aye, aye, Captain." Geneva mock-salutes him and heads back into the wheelhouse.

I look up at Harley and catch his eye. This time I notice he looks away first. He starts another lap.

Huh. I shake my head. Harley. Afraid of me. That's a laugh. Because now I know who he reminds me of. Minus the booze, Harley's just like my dad.

—/—

We are back out again. Me and the rest of the crew of the *Miranda Lee*. My crew. I like the sound of that. More backbreaking work, but the rhythm and the pain of it are sweet. Cold fingers and tired arms never felt so good. It's like I'm building a house or something. Like I'm building a home. The days blend into one sweaty, cold, bait-scented blur, but for the first time since Bar died I'm actually happy. It's starting to feel like my life, finally. Not my dad's, and not Lucy the Giant's, but mine. Just me.

We catch our load and head back toward the processing plant. But this time Harley chugs right past the old barge and keeps on toward the distant shore.

"That's it for the king crab, hon," Geneva tells me. "We've got downtime for at least a few weeks until the Tanner crab season opens. Harley'll sell this back in Kodiak, then we'll all settle in town for a while."

In town. The words register. "You mean, like, live? Off the boat?" My heart sinks. Somehow I had imagined staying on the *Miranda Lee* indefinitely. Instead, I'm right back where I started—stuck in Kodiak without a place to stay. Geneva reads my mind.

"Well, you can't exactly stay *here*. Don't worry," she says, patting my shoulder, "there are plenty of rooms for rent. Let's see. Who do I know? Oh, what about Cap'n George? You and that big dog of his hit it off pretty well. Maybe George can help you out."

"Thanks, Geneva." I still feel nervous. You can't fool all the people all the time, right? Every day in Kodiak is a day someone could figure out who I am. Maybe if I can find the guts to talk to Harley, I can ask him if I could stay on board the boat instead.

Geneva leaves and I realize I'm holding my breath. I exhale slowly. It's still a long way to shore.

It's six o'clock in the morning when we pull into the harbor. In summer it'd look like high noon just about now, but in mid-February the sun is nowhere in sight. In the bunkroom, I pack what little I own into my backpack. It feels a lot like my first night in Kodiak. I take a deep breath. Time to talk to Harley.

Before I can turn around, Harley taps on the doorframe. He's found me first. "You can keep your survival suit on board, if you want, until we go out again. Or I can help you carry it when you find a place."

"Uh, no. No, I'll leave it here." My tongue knots up again. Harley rubs the back of his head and looks away. Geneva was right. We make each other nervous.

"Okay." He nods and leaves.

That went well. At least I have an excuse to come back later on. Maybe I can talk to him then. Maybe.

Above deck, Tracer's already jumped ship and I can hear him whooping his way up the pier to the nearest bar. Geneva comes out on deck behind us.

"Galley's all cleaned up, Harley. Nothing left out to spoil while we're gone but yourself."

"Thanks, Gen. I guess I'll see you in a few."

"Or sooner," Geneva says, and gives me a sly wink. "Barbara's invited us all over to dinner as soon as she gets settled in."

"What?" I exclaim. I can already see me dishing out bowls of instant oatmeal and crystallized raisins. My specialty. "I can't cook! And I don't even have a place yet!"

"Oh, don't be so modest, Barb. Besides, you said it yourself. Just because you're new in town, there's no point in being completely alone."

My mouth is hanging open, but I get the hint. Harley, however, glares at Geneva.

"I don't think I can make—" Harley starts to say.

"Of course you can make it," Geneva scolds. "Even Don's gonna be there, so quit hemming, or you'll hurt Barb's feelings." Harley closes his mouth, stunned. Geneva turns to me.

"Well? Didn't you have something to ask him?"

I *want* to ask him to help me throw Geneva overboard. Instead, I say, "What . . . what do you like to eat?" My voice squeaks a bit on the last word, but no one seems to notice. Harley darts Geneva a doubtful look.

"Oh, I don't know. Anything with gravy, I guess. No more crab."

"Great." Geneva grins. "Sounds like turkey to me. A regular postholiday dinner with all the trimmings."

"What!" I scream, but Harley actually seems to be warming to the idea. Surprisingly, so am I. I haven't had a real turkey dinner since my mom left. If only I could pull it off. "What—what time is good for you guys?" I stammer.

"I don't know," Harley says slowly. He's watching both of us now, but he's stopped giving Geneva the evil eye. "Why don't you get settled in first, then let us all know. Geneva knows where to find me."

"Terrific!" I say, and my voice goes up an octave on the terrified squeak scale.

"Come on." Geneva taps my shoulder and tosses her stuff down to the pier. I climb down after her and wave a weak goodbye to Harley and the *Miranda Lee*. After *my* cooking, who knows if I'll see either one of them again.

"What are you trying to do to me?" I say through clenched teeth when Geneva and I reach the street.

"Hon, you looked half sick at the thought of leaving the boat. I thought you could use some company. And it's high time that skipper of ours got over his fear of friendship. It'll be fine. I'll even help you cook, if you want me to."

"Do I ever. Last meal I cooked was day-old McDonald's in the microwave. And I burned that."

Geneva lets out a breath. "Well, then I guess it'll keep us both off the streets and busy for a little while. But first we've got to get you a place to sleep." Geneva winks at me again and I have to forgive her. But I can't believe I ever compared her to a fairy godmother. Cinderella would've run screaming for the hills with help like this.

Geneva takes me to a place called Harborside Coffee just south of the harbor. Cap'n George is seated in a booth by the window. The captain must be a regular here, because Killit looks right at home stuffed under the table. The big dog thumps his tail on the ground when he sees us.

"Back so soon?" Cap'n George asks, rising from his table.

"Don't act so surprised." Geneva laughs and sweeps him into a hug.

"Hey, Killit." I squat down to give the big dog a scratch behind the ears. He solemnly scoots forward on his belly to give me better access. I love this dog.

The captain leans over the table. "So how was your first round out there?"

"I liked it." Killit thumps his tail.

"Glad to hear it. Can I get you some coffee?"

"No," Geneva responds before I can even open my mouth. "What this lady here needs is a room. And I'm thinking you've got just the place for her, seeing as how Killit approves and all."

Once again I have no idea what's going on. Geneva has a habit of launching into negotiations before I even know we're at the table, I'm discovering. But it's always in my best interest, so this time I keep my mouth shut.

"Does he now?" Cap'n George asks with a raised eyebrow. He nudges Killit under the table with his shoe. "What do you think, Killit? A new boarder for a few weeks?"

I can hardly believe it when Killit whimpers in response. It even sounds a bit like a yes. The captain laughs and shakes his head. "That one always was a sucker for a good chest scratch," he says, grinning. "Welcome aboard. The place isn't much, but it's warm, roomy enough, and has a good stove. Order up

some lunch and then I'll take you up there to see for yourself."

"Thank you, sir." Cap'n George puffs up a little at the *sir*.

"I like this woman," he tells Geneva.

"Well, I guess it all works out then," she replies, and calls the waitress over to order the halibut special.

After lunch, Geneva, the captain, Killit, and I climb what must be the steepest hill in all of Kodiak to reach the Victorian house that the captain calls home. There are even wooden stairs built into the hillside to help you climb straight to the top instead of following the winding road. "The place isn't much" is the understatement of the century, I realize. This house is amazing. All lacy woodwork and bright colors that seem somehow out of place in the snowy roughness of the town, but it is beautiful to me. There's no way I can afford to live here.

"Damn fool thing to build a Victorian in this climate, and I'm half crazy trying to keep the gingerbread on when the snows hit hard," the captain grumbles. He reaches up and snaps off a dangling piece of the woodwork overhanging the front porch like icing from a witch's house. "But it keeps me busy. Makes me feel almost useful."

He scrapes his feet on the welcome mat. "Well, come on in. I'll make some tea."

Cap'n George's home is even prettier on the inside. Honey-colored wood and fancy carpets everywhere. There's even a big brass spyglass in the bay window overlooking the town and the harbor. It's like being on one of those turn-of-the-century luxury ships, like the *Titanic,* but high on a hill instead. Living here might work out after all. But then again, I haven't even gotten my first paycheck yet.

"Living room, dining room, kitchen, parlor," the captain says, giving us a tour of the ground floor. The parlor looks a lot like the living room, but one has books and the other an old TV. The rooms stretch on for miles, and the ceilings are twice as high as any I've ever seen. This house actually seems to fit me. I can feel my smile stretching wider and wider as we move through the first floor. At the staircase, the captain looks up. "Your room would be upstairs, in the attic," he announces.

My smile drops. The attic. Again. I take a step back. My big horizons shrink back to Sitka-sized agony.

"I can't afford this," I whisper to Geneva. It's probably true, but I'm also hoping it'll save me from living in yet another attic.

Geneva reads my mind. She punches my arm.

"Oh, don't look so glum until you see it," she tells me. "Cap'n, what're you asking?"

Cap'n George scratches his head beneath his hat. "Well, I don't know. Place is pretty much paid for, and it's true Killit and I could use the company."

"Better than playing bingo down at the VA," Geneva pipes in.

Cap'n George scowls at her. "Be that as it may, I don't believe in a free ride. Let's say three hundred dollars for the month. And you make your own bed."

Geneva cocks an eye at me. "You can't beat that. My sister charges me five hundred, and she's family." She winks and turns to the captain. "We don't get paid until tomorrow."

The captain waves his hand. "Fine, fine. We'll worry about that after you get settled in. Why don't you ladies head on up and take a look around? I'll put the water on."

Geneva's right. I'll never find another place like this, or another landlord as nice as Cap'n George. Deal with it, Lucy, I tell myself. Living in an attic isn't exactly the end of the world.

Killit leads the way up the first flight of stairs. "George is a good man. You'll like it here. His bedroom is back there," Geneva says, pointing to a half-opened door at the top of the stairs. "Runs the length of the house and gives him a view of the water." We walk the hallway to an open room. The reading room, Geneva calls it, although all the books seem to be downstairs. Instead, this place is full of charts and maps. But I guess you can read those, too.

Up the next flight of stairs is a tiny little landing. Killit beats us to it and waits, wagging his tail impatiently. I can hear the stairs creak under my feet, and the ceiling seems to get lower and lower the closer I get to the top of the staircase.

There's a plain wooden door on the side of the landing. "Go on," Geneva urges. I don't know why I'm hesitating. I take a deep breath and open the door.

The captain's attic is a fairy tale. The ceiling rises eight feet above my head in wonderful peaks that I realize follow the shape of the rooftop. The room is a giant U shape, not as large as the first floor, but full of little windows and the rich smell of cedar planking. Suddenly I can't imagine staying on the *Miranda Lee* in dock, not by a long shot.

"Geneva, it's perfect!"

"I know. I'd stay here myself if my sister didn't get after me to spend time with her and her kids."

"I thought she charged you rent?"

"Oh, she does, but we barter it out in baby-sitting

time." She grins and looks around the room. "George has a sense of the dramatic, but you've got to admit it's a nice space to live in."

Without thinking, I sweep Geneva into a big bear hug.

"Careful, don't want to break me," she laughs, but she hugs me right back. Killit leaps up on both of us, wanting to join in the fun. It's not until after I put Geneva down and give Killit his own well-deserved hug that I realize I'm crying.

"What's wrong, honey?"

"Nothing." My voice catches in my throat.

"Well, it must be something. Bed too small? Allergic to dogs?"

"No, no, no. Nothing like that. The bed is terrific. I've never slept in a bed that big. And Killit's the best. It's just . . . everything's so great. It's never been this way for me before."

Geneva's face softens, and once again I'm reminded of a fairy godmother. "Well, Barbara, maybe it's high time it was."

The moment is almost perfect. But the name isn't mine. I'm seized with the urge to tell her everything—my age, where I come from, how I got here. But most of all, I want to tell her my name.

"Lucy," I finally say in a whisper. "It's Lucy."

But Geneva doesn't hear me. She's already headed back down the stairs.

"Cap'n, she'll take it," she hollers down the stairwell. "And oh, you're invited to dinner next week right here in the dining room. Barb says she's making a holiday feast for the crew."

Killit looks up at me with those big brown eyes of his and I can't help smiling.

"Hear me, boy? My name is Lucy. And you can come to dinner too. Just as soon as I learn how to cook."

Killit wags his tail and licks my hand, and somehow everything is still pretty great.

CHAPTER 9

February 20

KODIAK, ALASKA

An hour ago Harley dropped off my first paycheck. It's been sitting on the sideboard in the hallway ever since. An embarrassing amount of money, really. Bigger than any of the government checks my dad ever got in the mail. Much bigger than the pile of cash on the table before one of his binges. I could pay my rent for a year and still send Sheila to college on a few of these paychecks. But it just sits there in the hallway because I can't even touch it. Checks don't mean zip if you don't have a bank account. Or if the check's made out to Barbara, and your name is Lucy.

I've been sitting on the staircase puzzling over this for a half hour when the captain comes home with Killit. Cap'n George doesn't go to work. He doesn't need to. People in Kodiak work for him. So he spends his semi-retirement, as he calls it, visiting people and piecing back together whatever little bits of trim fall off his house.

"Any luck?" I ask as he comes through the door. The captain's been in town all morning trying to find the right shade of lilac paint for the window frames.

"Not hardly," he grunts, and hangs his hat on a peg. "Nobody in this town has an eye for color. I'll have to send to Anchorage for it." He starts to shuffle through the mail on the table, then notices my paycheck.

"Not bad." He winks up at me. "Harley must've busted your humps over those pots of his to bring in that kind of haul, especially with the trouble he's been having lately. Maybe you're good luck." He grins at me again. I grin back, a bit weakly. I'd love to be somebody's good luck. But first I've got to be my own.

"So, you gonna cash it, or you just gonna sit there looking at it? First paycheck's always pretty enough to frame, but it's more fun to spend." He chuckles to himself and stomps off to the kitchen.

I take a deep breath and follow him.

"Cap'n . . . ?"

"Yeah?"

"I . . . can't cash my check. I know I owe you rent money, and Geneva's gonna be here in an hour to go shopping for dinner and all, but . . ."

"What?" He raises an eyebrow and pauses over the coffee he's pouring.

"Well . . . I don't have a bank to cash it at."

"Is that all? Sign it over to me. I'll cash it for you."

"Really?" I almost get excited. But then the name thing gets in the way.

"I mean, no, I couldn't . . . impose like that."

Cap'n George shrugs. "It's up to you. Of course, you could always ask Harley to write it out to cash and take it to his bank down on Front Street."

"You can do that?" How come nobody tells kids these things? There should be a book or something on how to be eighteen and over.

"Little lady, you can do anything you want," he tells me. And suddenly I'm so happy I almost knock the poor man over with a hug. Check in one hand, jacket in the other, I race off to find Harley so I can get back in time to shop for supper.

It's another one of those rare sunny afternoons in Kodiak, but cold and brittle as an icicle. I shove my hands deeper into my pockets and jog down the steps to the harbor. I don't know where Harley lives when we're in town. It seems like he hardly ever leaves the *Miranda Lee*. Geneva and even Tracer have family hereabouts, and now I have Killit and the captain. But

Harley, well, like me, Harley seems to have his own secrets to keep.

"Permission to come aboard," I call out, pounding down the pier.

"Hey, Barb," Harley calls back without even looking up to see who it is. He's coiling rope on deck, the cuffs of his thick green sweater tucked into a pair of work gloves. "You sound like Monroe beating up those planks," he says, and gives me a small smile. "What's up?"

I don't even stop to catch my breath. "Harley, I need my check in cash. I don't have a bank out here and it'll be easier for me all around." I take a deep breath and stand there, arms folded. Then unfolded, then folded again. I'm not sure which will make me look more certain of myself. But if he says no, I don't know what I'll do. I stand a little taller, but then I realize Harley is staring at me. I lose my bravado and slump again.

"Okay. Give me a minute." Harley hops up, wipes his hands on his jeans, and goes into the wheelhouse. I can't believe it.

He comes back a couple of minutes later with a check even more beautiful than the last because this one says *Payable to Cash* and I know that finally I am on my home-free, earned-it-myself way.

"Uh, how much do I owe you for my sleeping bag and stuff?"

Harley squints up at me from the pile of ropes he's coiling. "Huh? Oh. Already paid up."

"Really?"

Harley gives me an amused look. "Really."

"Well, thanks. Okay. See you tomorrow at eight," I call behind me, already halfway back to the wharf. First thing I'm doing when I get home is cut my dad's old credit card up into tiny bits. Barb the Adult is on her way.

I turn around and wave to Harley again. "Thank you!" I shout. For the first time, Harley breaks into a bona fide grin. He shakes his head and goes back to work. And I whoop it up on the inside, taking the stairs up the hill to the captain's house in twos, like Tracer going for a beer after a week on the waves.

"Good Lord! Cap'n, will you talk some sense into this woman?" Geneva stands in the doorway of my bedroom, jaw practically on the floor. I freeze like a deer in the middle of the road and glance around. Everything seems normal. Adult. Fine.

Geneva is looking at my pay, stacked in even piles of cash on the dresser by the door.

"Don't you at least have a wallet?" she asks incredulously.

"What for?"

"Honey, I don't know where you're from, but in Kodiak we don't leave heaping piles of money on top of the furniture. Jesus, Barb, that's three weeks' worth of work. At least put it in a cookie jar."

"Oh . . . okay." So much for using Dad as a role model. Banks, Lucy. Normal people use banks.

"Well then." Geneva rubs her hands together. "Count out enough for shopping. We've got to get a move on if the turkey's going to be defrosted by tomorrow."

I pocket a few bills and slide the rest of my money into the top drawer with my underwear and socks. Tomorrow I guess I'll buy a cookie jar.

It's starting to drizzle when we climb into the old jeep Geneva drives when she's in town. During the rest of the year she keeps it at her sister's place.

"God, kids grow up so fast, it seems," she tells me as we plow through the icy streets. The roads are crystallized with a month's worth of snowstorms, and today's drizzle isn't going to help. "My sister's little boy looked like he was about five years old last year. Now he's almost as tall as I am."

Geneva's not that tall, so I have to ask. "How old is he?"

"Tommy? Well, he's got to be eleven now, why?"

I shake my head. "I was your size when I was nine."

Geneva snorts a little laugh. "Nobody pulled *your* pigtails, I'll bet."

"They couldn't reach them." I'm dead serious, but this makes Geneva laugh even harder.

"Barb, you're too much."

The thought of Geneva standing knee-high to her nephew and nieces makes me laugh. "You ever think about having a family?"

Geneva smiles. "I don't have kids of my own, but there's my sister's family, and Harley and Don and George. And you. That's all the family I need."

I have to swallow before I can talk again. "That's the nicest thing anyone's ever said to me."

Geneva pats my hand. "Well, good."

We drive on in silence, Geneva with her eyes on the road, and me trying my best not to cry.

Instead of pulling into the grocery store parking lot, Geneva passes it up for a strip mall.

"First order of business for any woman of sound mind—something to wear." She parks the jeep in front of a little boutique that boasts SIZES FOR EVERY WOMAN.

"Before I found this place, I used to have to shop in the kids' section at Carr's for skirts. Petites and Pluses, this place has it all."

She hops out of the jeep, but I hesitate. Shopping. We're really going shopping.

"Coming, Barb? I mean, correct me if I'm wrong, but you've only got the clothes on your back and more of the same at home, right? You want to wear jeans for the rest of your life?"

I start to argue, but she's got a point. This is your life now, Lucy girl. Make the most of it. I follow her into the store.

I hate shopping. Back in Sitka I either had to buy men's clothes or maternity wear for most things. Or dig around in boxes for fuzz-covered sweaters. Not exactly high fashion. But inside the boutique there are almost too many things to choose from.

"Don't worry. I'll walk you through it," Geneva says. For the next half hour I hide behind the curtain of my little dressing room, trying on a dozen different outfits.

"Let me see, hon," Geneva calls. I've got one leg out of a miniskirt and have to hop to keep my balance.

"No." I look ridiculous. Tina Martin would die laughing.

"What's wrong with it?"

"It's too . . . leggy."

"Hon, that's what legs are for."

"Not my legs." In the mirror they look like tree trunks. I can almost hear my dad—"Christ Almighty! Look at them redwoods!" My face gets hot just thinking about it. Even if I had to cook dinner by myself, it'd be better than this.

I pull my jeans back on and step outside the dressing room. "Can we go now?"

"One more thing." She shoves a dress into my arms and pushes me back through the curtain.

"Geneva . . ."

"Just put it on. I'm not letting you leave until you do."

I could sob. Instead, I suck it up and pull the dress on over my clothes. I look at myself in the mirror. What I see makes me pull off my pants and put the dress on for real.

It's velvet. Long and soft, in a deep wine color that makes my skin look caramel-brown. It's beautiful.

"You're awfully quiet," Geneva says, yanking the curtain aside.

"Hey! I could've been naked!"

"But you're not. Come out where I can see you."

I hesitate, then step outside. The three-way mirror confirms it. Lucy the Giant looks good in a dress.

I take a deep breath.

"You like it?" Geneva asks.

"I like it."

She smiles and gives me a little punch on the arm. "Then good. Now let's get going. We've got a dinner to cook."

The captain's kitchen seems bigger somehow with a big old raw turkey sitting in the middle of it and bags of groceries all over the place.

"Don't let it intimidate you," Geneva says, and slaps an apron into my hands.

"The first rule of cooking is timing. Start the big things first, the things that take longest, like the bird. Figure it out so it's all ready at the same time. The second rule is clean as you go. Nothing worse than sitting down to a big dinner, then having bowls and counters to clean up after you're done. And it only gets worse if you wait until morning.

"So." Geneva takes point at the head of the counter. She conducts me with a wooden spoon. "Finish unpacking those bags. Refrigerate the perishables, and take a stick of butter out of the freezer while you're at it so it's soft by tomorrow. We'll thaw the turkey tonight, peel and chop the potatoes, and put together the pie. It'll be your job tomorrow to put the oven on three-fifty and put the turkey in, I'd say by one o'clock. Potatoes and veggies go on at seven-thirty, pie goes in about eight-ten. Should have just enough time to cool by the time we're done eating at nine or so. Okay?"

I'm still fumbling with the apron strings—how do you tie things behind your back? But I nod. "Great."

"Oh, there's enthusiasm for you. Don't worry, Barb, you're in good hands. Now let's get to work."

Cooking is not easy. Well, it is if you don't think about it and you have someone helping you do it. But it's a lot of work. I have new respect for Vickie Drake and all of the other kids behind the counter at McDonald's. Of course, they just deep-fry their little premade apple pies. I actually have to peel the apples myself, cover them in lemon juice so they don't go brown, and make the crust, too. Well, actually, the apples go brown anyway, and I let Geneva make the crust. But I pinch it all together and set it in the fridge for the next day.

We work into the night, and finally eat a couple of Geneva's awesome salmon omelets before calling it a day.

The next morning I'm up at six-fifteen.

"The oven only takes a few minutes to heat up," Cap'n George tells me when he comes down for coffee. So I cut it off and come back later. And then I remember. "Gravy," I say out loud. "It's the one thing Harley asked for and I forgot to ask Geneva how to make it."

"You need to wait for the turkey first, then use the drippings," the captain says from behind the morning paper. So I wait for the turkey. But it's not even supposed to go into the oven until one. So I pace instead.

"You're making me nervous," Cap'n George finally says. "I feel like I'm in a waiting room. Here." He tosses me my coat. "Take Killit for a run. *I'll* put the bird in if you don't get back in time."

I collapse onto the sofa. "I'm sorry, I'm just . . . I just want everything to be perfect tonight."

"Well, it won't be. Nothing ever is. So stop worrying about it and enjoy yourself."

I grab a pillow and hug it hard. "Some things can be perfect," I say. "Everything's been perfect for me here."

"Perfection and Kodiak rarely go hand in hand."

I sigh and rest my cheek on the pillow. Killit settles by my feet and rests his head on my knee. "See that?" I point out to the captain. "Perfect."

"You, my dear lady, are exceedingly easy to please. Another good trait." He folds his paper and his voice softens. "Barbara. We're very glad to have you here. Things have been tough on the *Miranda Lee* crew for some time now, and it looks like the trouble is finally easing up. It doesn't take a rocket scientist to guess that you've been through a tough time or two yourself.

Enjoy the break, and enjoy your friends. There'll be plenty of things to worry about when the time is right. Gravy isn't one of them."

Killit thumps his tail in agreement and I have to laugh. I wish I'd had a grandfather like Cap'n George. But I've got something better—I've got the man himself. I give the captain a kiss on the head and he pats my hand.

"See," I tell him. "Perfect."

Just when it seems like the day will never end, seven-thirty rolls around and it's time to make the gravy. I stand over the pan, mashing little balls of flour into the sauce with the back of a spoon.

"It looks lumpy."

"It's fine," Geneva says over her shoulder.

"It's not brown enough."

"It's fine, hon. We'll start over if we need to. Just relax."

Gravy. You have to do so much to get it right—brown the flour in oil, add water, but not too fast or it'll get lumpy, but it can't be too soupy either. I hate it.

"Honey, go get dressed," Geneva orders me. "Everything else is done. Table's set. The punch is done. You did a wonderful job, but you look a mess."

I look down at myself—covered in flour, slop, and

bits of grease. I look like a cafeteria wall after a food fight.

"Jeez. Why didn't you tell me?"

"I said clean as you go, hon. You've got to start listening to me. Go get dressed. I'll make the gravy."

"But—"

"No buts, just do it. Don't worry. I'll tell everyone you made it yourself. They'll be very proud."

I give Geneva a quick kiss on the cheek. I wonder if my mother would have been like her. But I guess not, because then she'd still be around, right?

"You're the best." And I run to go get dressed. Who knew dinner parties could be such an ordeal?

I'm so nervous I have to pee. So I run to the bathroom, but I'm too stressed to use it. Instead, I fidget with my hair in the mirror and check my dress for flour stains. My holiday hostess dress, Geneva calls it. I have to admit it is pretty. Even my dad would have a hard time putting it down. Not that he wouldn't try. As far as I'm concerned, all the Tina Martins and Charlotte Bakers of the world can keep their size-three shopping buddies. I've got Geneva now.

After tugging at my dress a few more times, I hunt down a tube of lipstick Geneva kept trying to push on me all afternoon, and I actually put some on.

And take it off.

And put it on again. Then the doorbell rings and I'm stuck wearing it because the guests are here and dinner is ready and I'm in my holiday hostess dress, and guess what, Lucy girl, it's show time.

The captain beats me to the door. He looks dashing in a tweed jacket. He's stoked the fire in the parlor and is even smoking a pipe.

"Welcome aboard, Harley," he says, and throws the door wide.

I tense up and wait for the verdict. *Lucy, you look like a Christmas tree. . . .*

Instead, Harley takes one look at me and smiles.

"Yep, she cleans up pretty nice," the captain says to him with a chuckle. I feel myself blush. Harley nods. Charlotte Baker, eat your heart out.

Harley's cleaned up too. His hair's slicked back and he's wearing a light blue button-down under a beautiful navy blue sweater that puts my old knotty pullover to shame.

"Now, this I've gotta see," says a voice outside the door. Harley steps aside as Don hobbles up the last step on a pair of metal crutches.

"Don!" I shout, and throw my arms around him in a big hug.

"Easy now. The old man breaks easily," he laughs.

"Sorry." I loosen my grip and help him inside.

"You do look good, Barb." He nods. Just then, Geneva comes whirling in from the kitchen.

"Pick up your jaws, boys, and have a seat in the parlor." Geneva's wearing a wild bright yellow pantsuit with bangley jewelry, and a little baking apron. She holds another one out to me. "Back to it, missy, bird's calling for you."

"Speaking of old birds." Don winks at Geneva.

"Watch it," she warns him, and returns the wink before whisking me away to the kitchen again.

"Glad you wore the lipstick," she says as the door swings shut behind us. My palms are sweating, but I realize I'm glad too. "It helps to remind them we're still women under all that fish. Grab the hors d'oeuvres over there. I'll pour the punch."

It's not until we sit down to dinner, with the table all laid out in the captain's best china, crystal shimmering in the candlelight, turkey steaming on a huge platter just like a picture from a magazine, that I finally relax. There's nothing left to do but the eating, as Geneva says. And I, Lucy, did it. I pulled it off.

"It smells good," Harley says. And I can see him eyeing the gravy. Geneva smiles.

"Better than hospital food," Don adds.

I blush. "Thanks. Um . . . Cap'n George . . . would you say grace?"

"I'd be glad to." I think the captain's enjoying his role as host. "I haven't had a full house in quite a while."

We all bow our heads and the captain speaks. "Bless this food we are about to receive from the bounty of Christ our Lord, and bless these fine people around this table for being who they are. A fine crew, a fine bunch of friends. Amen."

"Amen," we all chime in. The captain rises to carve the bird, and if this was a movie the violins would start in with something happy and seasonal and we'd all laugh and toast and make merry. My heart feels like it's swelling. Like I'm Little Orphan Annie and I've just found my new home.

Then Harley looks up and says, out of the blue, "Didn't you invite Tracer?"

CHAPTER 10

February 21

KODIAK, ALASKA

If this was a movie, the film would snap. It would bubble up and burn all brown and blue like those crappy old filmstrips in science class. I can actually *feel* the silence at the table. How could I have forgotten Tracer?

"See, Barb, nothing's perfect." Cap'n George shrugs with a sympathetic smile. "Don't worry. We'll get on the horn and give him a call."

"But it *was* perfect," I tell him. Then I realize that not having Tracer here to spoil it—that's perfect too.

But it isn't right. Tracer dislikes me enough already. I've been the odd man out too many times not to know I'd never want to make someone else feel that way. Especially now that I've got a better life.

Geneva pats my hand. "Don't look so worried,

honey. We'll get him here. We won't even eat till he shows up, if it helps."

I twist my napkin in my hands. "Sorry, everybody." I push my chair back from the table. "Does anyone have his number?"

We try the boardinghouse where Tracer sometimes stays on his downtime, but he's not there.

"Try his dad's," Geneva suggests. Harley dials the number and I take the receiver. It rings and rings.

"Ah, his old man's probably passed out, can't get to the phone," Geneva says in annoyance. "Tracer's probably hitting the bars himself. Don't worry about it, Barb. It was an honest mistake. We'll save him some pie."

We sit back down to dinner, but the movie feeling is gone for good and I feel even worse. Tracer's got a bum dad like me. Maybe he needs a new family as much as I do.

Geneva takes over as hostess, keeping everyone happy, glasses full, and chatting about who knows what. I'm not listening really. Maybe the captain is right. Nothing's perfect. Least of all me.

"It's called responsibility," Cap'n George says when I hop up from the table and grab my coat. I can hear Bar's dream voice echoing the same thing. *Responsibility.* Time to grow up.

"It's called worrying about nothing," Geneva

grouses, but she helps me pack a plate with all the trimmings, just the same. "Tracer gets on my last nerve, and he harps on you like there's no tomorrow as it is. But I suppose if he finds out about tonight, we'll never hear the end of it."

"Thanks, Geneva," I say, and give her a hug. She hugs me back. "Now get going before that plate gets cold."

Harley is waiting for me in the hallway, wearing his coat.

"Two are better than one," he says, and opens the door.

"Call us when you find him," Geneva shouts. She stands in the doorway with the captain and waves. The night blows cold and wet around us as we descend the hill to the Polar Bar and all the other usual haunts on the waterfront.

Food doesn't stay warm long on a winter night in Alaska. By the time we've checked all the bars and restaurants, Tracer's dinner plate is starting to ice over in my hands.

"What about the boat?" I ask Harley. He shrugs and we tromp to the end of the pier.

The *Miranda Lee* glows, warm and inviting, bobbing gently in its slip.

"Tracer?" I call, and run on ahead. The light is on in the galley, and there are dishes lying in the sink.

But Tracer is nowhere to be found. Harley is waiting for me in the bunkroom.

"No luck," I tell him. "But *somebody's* been living here."

"Uh . . . that would be me," Harley says with a little wave of his hand.

"What?"

Harley shrugs. "I prefer it that way. Come on, I'll put on some tea. We're not going to find Tracer this late if he doesn't want to be found."

I take a seat at the galley table. Harley puts water on, then rummages through the cupboard for mugs. Watching him, I feel like I'm on the *Miranda Lee* for the first time. This time it's not just a boat, it's someone's house.

"You know, before Geneva introduced me to Cap'n George, I wanted to ask if I could stay out here. But I guess I'm not the only one who considers the boat home."

Harley turns around and smiles, the tea mugs found. He pours me a cup in the one that says SKIPPER on the side.

"I've been calling the *Miranda Lee* home for more years than I care to remember," he confesses. "Not exactly a houseboat, but it suits me. Hell, tonight and payday were big trips inland for me."

I take a sip of tea—warm and cinnamony orange

spice. I can feel it all the way down to my toes. I feel like I've come home.

"Honey?" Harley asks.

"Yes?" My head snaps up. "I mean, what?"

Harley grins and points at my cup. "Do you want honey with that, or sugar?"

I feel myself blush. "Oh. Thanks. Honey's good." Stupid, Lucy. Really dumb. Harley's your skipper, not your dad. Still, when I see the honey jar is almost empty, I'm careful not to tell him he needs to go shopping.

I try to change the subject. "Do you have family on shore?"

Harley sits across from me with a sigh. He sounds tired. Sad, like the humpbacks surfacing in the channel back home. "No one that wants to see me," he says. "My ex-wife, Maggie, is Inuit. She came up here from Southeastern, near Ketchikan."

"My mother was Haida," I offer. When he looks at me, I have to look away. Lucy's mom was Haida. But I'm Barb now. I don't have a mom. "But I didn't really know her," I add. That part, at least, is true.

Harley smiles again, slow and sad. "Yeah. I guess I didn't know Maggie, either. We got married too young. Work was hard. I took to crabbing at sea and drinking on shore. Needless to say, it didn't work out. She went back to her family."

For the first time, Harley is opening up to me. And I can't do the same. Not if I want to stay. But I can't make myself stop listening, either. I try to picture him sitting in McDonald's with my dad, red-eyed and hungover. Instead, I see him looking at me, his face hollowed out with misery. That same sad look he gave me at the Polar Bar my first night in town. The night I got drunk. And I know I must look that way too. Harley's story isn't a new one. It could be my parents', but for the ending.

I feel like I'm trespassing. This is a conversation for grown-ups. Not for a kid like me. A kid who's pretending to be somebody else. Suddenly I want to explain myself to him, at least part of the way. "Harley, remember when you said we all have demons to wrestle? My dad . . . well, I know how I must've looked that night at the bar. But I just grew up around drinkers. I didn't become one."

Harley smiles and looks down at his cup. "I know, Barb. I know you now. It's funny. Sometimes you make a lot of mistakes when you're young, and it's supposed to be okay. Chalk it up to lack of experience. But people still get hurt."

Am I hurting anybody? I wonder. My father, who never speaks to me? My mother, who's been gone longer than she stayed? It seems to me I've got no one left to hurt in Sitka, even if I wanted to. And I'd never do anything to ruin what I have here in Kodiak. People hurt each other more often than not, I guess. But how many of them get a chance to understand?

"Do you still love her?" I ask. "Your wife?"

Harley laughs, an ugly sound, like a fox barking in the night. It reminds me of my dad.

"Sorry. I shouldn't have asked." Prying, Lucy, you're prying. I stand up and start washing the dishes in the sink to cover my nervousness. Don't go looking for answers that aren't there, Luce. It's not smart.

There's no hot water in the galley—it's too precious to use for anything but showers. My hands get cold fast.

Harley joins me. "Don't be sorry, Barb. I brought it up. Here." He takes a plate from me and rinses it. "You wash, I'll rinse and dry."

I'm afraid to look up, but I do. "Okay."

Harley gives me a warm smile. He grabs a dish towel from a drawer.

"As far as love goes, that was all a long time ago. When I think about Maggie at all these days, it's because I'm thinking about our little girl, Miranda."

I feel like I've just been jabbed by a hundred hot little pins. "Miranda *Lee*?" Harley has a little girl somewhere. A daughter of his own. I can't believe it.

"Yep, the real Miranda Lee." His face goes soft in a way my dad's never does. "The court said if I could keep up on my child-support payments, clean myself up, maybe I'd get to see her again. But I fell off the wagon a few times, and stayed behind on everything.

"Then one day I ended up with the *Miranda Lee*. She's Cap'n George's old boat, you know. I live out here to stay out of trouble. I don't pay rent. I finally paid her off last year. Now, what I make this season, I keep. And maybe next year, if the haul's good, I'll get to see my little girl.

"Maybe that's why I love this boat so much," he says, more to himself than to me. "I haven't seen Randi in almost six years. I wouldn't even know what she looks like now." He falls silent and I sit there, stunned. Six years. Six years he's worked, stayed sober, just to see his little girl again. That's the difference between my story and his. My dad is my dad. But Harley . . . he's something else.

"I didn't think people like you actually existed," I say quietly. Harley laughs self-consciously.

"Like me how?"

It takes me a minute to find the words. "People who change, I guess. People who care."

"Yeah, well. Let's just hope I've changed enough. And that our luck has changed for the better too. The season's not over yet."

I finish the last of the dishes and help Harley put

them away. I wonder if my father even knows I'm gone.

"Jeez." Harley stretches and groans. "Christmas came and went so fast. Hey, maybe you can tell me. What does a thirteen-year-old girl want for Christmas?"

My heart thumps in my throat. "I . . ." Thirteen. Just a couple years younger than me. And I know exactly what she would want. Harley leans forward in anticipation, but I can't look up when I say, "A mother who loves her enough to take her with her . . . and a dad like you."

I clear my throat and glance up. Harley is staring at me, his eyes bright.

"Well, it's getting late," I say quickly. I gather my coat and move toward the door. "I guess we won't be finding Tracer, after all. Do you want his dinner?"

Harley blinks like he's waking up; then he follows me. "Sure. It'll make a good breakfast."

"Well, good night then." I hesitate, wondering if it's okay to give my skipper a hug, when the tiny kitchen radio crackles to life.

"Hello!" Harley exclaims. He jogs to the radio and twists the dial for better reception. It's Fish and Game announcing that tomorrow at midnight, they're opening the next crab fishery.

"Looks like we're on again." Harley slaps his hands together. His face shines with excitement and I know it's more than just the thrill of being out again. Every day spent crabbing brings him that much closer to his little girl. A little shiver travels up my spine and spreads into a big grin.

"I'll go tell Geneva and the captain."

"Be here bright and early," Harley says, all business now. "Supplies are gonna be a bear to get tomorrow."

"Aye, aye, Skipper," I say with a mock salute, and make my way down to the dock.

"And Barb?" Harley calls after me. "Thanks."

My face turns red. "Don't thank me. Geneva did most of the cooking, really."

"No. I mean . . ." He trails off, and I realize I've embarrassed *him* for a change.

"Anytime."

I leave Harley standing on deck looking up at the stars.

My head is full of new information—daughters and houseboats and crabbing again. I'm halfway up the street before I notice that the door to the Polar Bar is open. Three guys come staggering out. The smell of too much booze bites the air. I wrap my scarf up higher, over my nose, and keep going. Then one of the men laughs. I know that laugh. I turn around. It's

Tracer, his arm wrapped around his new buddies—Coast Guard, still in their on-duty parkas.

"Tracer," I start to call, and stop.

One of the guys with Tracer seems familiar. I look closer. Not a face from Kodiak. He's from Sitka. Dan Devine. Sheila's older brother. The one who joined the Coast Guard.

At that exact moment Tracer sees me.

"Hey, Barb!" he shouts. Dan looks up too. He squints at me. I scurry back out of the lamplight, praying he's too drunk to recognize me. But my scarf can't do much to hide my size.

"Ah, that's right. Thinks she's too good for us," I hear Tracer mutter. "I heard about dinner!" he shouts after me. I run the hell out of there, as fast as I can.

"Honey, you look like you've seen a ghost." Geneva puts a hand to my cheek as I shrug off my coat. My heart is racing. I just want to hide, to fade away. Instead, I think of a convincing lie.

"No. I ran all the way back. Run's opening tomorrow night. Harley wants us in early. I'm tired. I need to go to bed."

"Sure thing, Barb. No luck with Tracer, huh?" I can't answer her. I just shake my head. "Well, Don's already gone home. Guess I'd better head out, too."

Geneva and I swap places at the coatrack and I give her a tight hug goodnight. "G'night, George," she calls into the parlor.

"Good night, Geneva. Dinner was wonderful," the captain replies. I lock the door behind Geneva and race up to my room, where I finally feel safe.

"He didn't recognize me," I tell Killit for the seventeenth time, huddled under the blankets of my bed. "I'll just lay low and stay out of the way until we set sail. Right, boy? It'll be all right."

Killit licks my hand as if he agrees with me. Everything will be all right.

That night, when I finally do fall asleep, I dream of my father sailing a ship named Lucy. Bar is still alive, and she plays in the front yard of the captain's house with Killit. She lives here along with Harley, Cap'n George, Geneva, and me.

Dan couldn't possibly know it was me.

Could he?

CHAPTER 11

February 22

KODIAK, ALASKA

It's five o'clock in the morning and the house is silent. I think if I can just lie here and be quiet it will stay this way, perfect, forever. I try to memorize every knot in the wooden beams of the ceiling. The way Killit looks, curled up on the little rug by the door. The pile of money on the dresser that never found its way to a bank. Five o'clock. I have to get moving, but I'm afraid to even get out of bed.

In the past month I've found a job, survived an ice storm, made new friends. I even have a home. Things Lucy the Giant couldn't even imagine, Barb the Adult has in spades. Barb has everything I ever wanted. Except a way to hold on to it all.

Dan will put two and two together and someone will be knocking on the door downstairs to take me away before the sun is even up. Until then, there's nothing else I can do.

Another half hour ticks by, and Killit whimpers in his sleep. His sides heave softly, and I think of Bar, out of breath, worn out, lying on my old bed. I have to squeeze my eyes shut to keep from crying.

And then there's a knock at the front door. It carries up the staircase to my attic. My heart skips a beat. Killit is instantly awake, scratching at my bedroom door, but I don't move to open it. Another knock. Killit looks at me and whimpers questioningly.

"Hush, Killit," I whisper. "Come here." He pads over and I slide off the bed to wrap my arms around him and wait. Downstairs, I can hear the captain wake up.

The house creaks as he makes his way to the first floor and opens the door. A woman is talking, but I can't make out what she is saying. They mount the stairs. Killit's eyes grow wide. I hold him back from the door. And then comes the knock, loud and certain. I can barely breathe.

"Rise and shine, Barb, or we'll leave withoutcha!"

Killit's tail thumps the ground. "Geneva?" My voice cracks.

"You decent?" She throws the door open without waiting for an answer.

"Hey, Gen," I say weakly. Geneva stomps into the

room in her work boots, takes one look at me and says, "Are you sick, hon? 'Cause the day's not getting any younger. We've got to get a move on if we're heading out today."

Relief floods through me and I sob. Killit nuzzles me, then jogs over to Geneva for a petting. I bury my face in my hands. Maybe Dan didn't know who I was, after all.

"Honey, what is it?" Geneva comes and sits next to me. My sobs turn to laughter.

"Nothing. I just . . . You didn't see anybody else outside, did you?"

"Sure I did, honey, the whole town. Now, are you going to tell me what this is about, or are you going to get dressed so we can get a move on?"

And then I realize how silly I've been. Thanks to Geneva, the whole town knows me as Barb. Barb the crabber. Barb who can drink a man under the table. Barb the Adult. That's me. From now on, that's who I am. Even if Dan thought he recognized me, every single person in Kodiak would tell him he's wrong.

"Thanks, Geneva." I give her a hug. She pats my back, a little bewildered.

"Anytime I can help without doing a thing, let me know. I'll wait downstairs."

After a quick shower I pack my work clothes and count out the money on the dresser. There's no time for a bank now, so I separate the money into two piles. One goes in my pocket, the other into an envelope along with a note to the captain asking him to keep it safe until I can open my own account. By the time I clunk down the stairs in my work boots, I feel lighter than I have in ages.

Geneva and Cap'n George are in the parlor having coffee. I poke my head inside. "Let me make a quick sandwich, then I'll be ready."

In the kitchen I pull out the turkey and stuffing and tuck my envelope of money at the back of the shelf for safekeeping. With all the food it's hiding behind, the captain might not find it at all and I can deal with it when I get back. I slap together some turkey and stuffing on toast with a little cranberry sauce, and grab my own cup of coffee. Killit bumps my leg with his nose, his tail wagging low. I grab a knife and split my sandwich in half to share with him.

"This is it, boy. I'll see you in a few weeks." I bury my face in Killit's thick fur. He makes a little squeaking sound through his nose. "I love you, Killit. I love everybody here. I'll be home soon."

Geneva joins me at the door with the captain. I pull on my parka and cap.

"Thank you for everything." I give Cap'n George a hug. He squeezes me back.

"Stay safe. Killit here'll get mad if you don't."

"Bye, George." Geneva gives him a peck on the cheek and we head out into the cold morning rain.

"There you are," Harley calls out when we reach the slip. "I was just about to give up on you guys."

"And what? Sail off to Tahiti?" Geneva asks with a wry smile. She tosses her duffel up to him and we climb aboard.

"Tracer's still a no-show, and you've been gone for an hour. Tahiti's not a bad option," Harley says with a grin. He gives me a wink. "Morning, Barb. Glad you could make it."

That wink hits me like a warm flood of happiness. "Sorry. I overslept."

"No problem," he says happily, and grabs our bags. "I'll put these in the bunkroom. Since it's just the three of us, I volunteer you ladies for supply duty."

"Thanks," Geneva mutters. And we turn right back around and head into town.

By midafternoon we have more cans of vegetables and boxes of macaroni and cheese than the stores do. I even make sure to buy an extra-large jar of honey. After stowing everything in the galley, I go back on deck to help Harley and Geneva with the last-minute checks on our traps and equipment. Being back on the *Miranda Lee* makes me feel at home again. A few of the other crabbers wave to me as they come and go along the pier. And every single one of them calls me Barb.

If I had any lingering doubts about Dan catching on to me, they fade as soon as Tracer shows up at the boat.

"Hey," he mumbles, and climbs on board. I turn around and it's like looking into the past. It's the same face I've seen every other day for the past ten years through the glass at McDonald's. My dad's—pasty-skinned, bleary-eyed and still half-drowned in whatever he was drinking the night before. Tracer stumbles past me with barely a glance.

"Hey," I say to his back, trying not to sound relieved. If Tracer's anything like my father, he's lucky he remembered where the *Miranda Lee* was docked this morning, let alone anything that might have happened last night.

"Well, look what the cat dragged in," Geneva says.

"Stow it," Tracer mutters, and goes into the wheelhouse.

"Oh, Harley's gonna love this," Geneva chuckles.

"Love what?" Harley asks from behind a crab pot.

"Our boy Tracer finally showed up. My guess is he's gonna try to sleep it off before reporting for duty."

"Great, just what I need." Harley climbs down from the pot. "I'll get him sobered up long enough to give him a talking-to." He rolls up his sleeves for emphasis and stomps into the wheelhouse.

I start to whistle. Geneva joins in. The way I figure it, Tracer'll have too much on his hands dealing with Harley in that mood to worry about anything to do with me. And I like it that way just fine.

"Want some coffee?" Harley asks me the next day. We've dropped the last set of traps and are motoring back to our first spot. The rain has let up for a little while. Harley joins me out on deck, watching the waves.

"Thanks."

The coffee is strong and hot, with lots of sugar, the way I like it. I wrap my gloves around the mug, grateful for the warmth.

"So. I spoke to my lawyer yesterday, before we left town." Harley's eyes are the same stormy gray as the water today. He keeps them focused on the horizon. "Looks like one, maybe two more runs like the last one and I'll be paid up on that child support. Might even get to see Miranda by the end of summer."

"That's great, Harley. That's . . . wow. You did it." I squeeze his hand before I can stop myself and he grins awkwardly.

"Yeah. Looks like I did. I just . . . wanted you to know."

He strolls off before I can say anything else. Now it's my turn to grin. I don't think I can get any happier than I am right now.

"Glad to see you two have stopped being so scared of each other," Geneva says, joining me at the railing. "Great news, huh?"

"The best. She's lucky to have a dad like him."

"And now she'll know it, too." Geneva nods. "How about you?"

"How about me what?"

"Whatever it was that made you go into the Polar Bar that night. Did it work out? Or should I still be worried about you?"

It's a good question. I probe around in my mind for the sore spots—my father, Bar, my mom. But it doesn't hurt so badly anymore. And that feels good. "No. I'm okay. I'm really okay."

Geneva pats me on the back. "Good. I like to see everybody happy. Especially my friends."

She gives me a quick hug, then points to the horizon. "Hey, look, the sun's coming out."

"Just in time," I say. And it is just in time for a glorious five-minute sunset over the waves, beneath a bank of gray-blue clouds.

"Enjoy it while we can," Geneva adds. We stroll up the deck to the bow, talking and laughing, and I'm thinking this is the best time I've ever had in my life. Harley is on the radio, talking to other skippers about weather and catches, deciding where to go next. Even Tracer is out of the way, perched in his favorite spot on top of the wheelhouse.

"Well, I've got to get supper started," Geneva finally says, and turns to go inside.

"Need any help?"

"Naw. Maybe later." She disappears into the galley.

The sun sets completely and twilight emerges through the little break in the clouds. I can see my future, bright and clean, like the icy waters around me. Things can change, Lucy girl. I'm a woman now. A woman with friends. Something, no, some*one*, I never thought I would be. The Bering spreads out before me like so much perfect snow and water. Ice floes drift here and there in the blue, blue waves. In the distance I can even see the dorsal fins of a pod of orca, breaching, leaping up and rolling to slap their backs on the water. They could be part of the same pod that travels through Sitka every year.

I strain to get a better look at them and try to hear their song.

"Hey, Giant!" somebody shouts.

Maybe because I'm thinking about Sitka, or maybe because, even now, the name still fits, I turn around. And in that instant I know I've given myself away.

"Hey, Lucy," Tracer says, grinning like a shark from his watchtower. "I thought that might be you."

CHAPTER 12

February 23

BERING SEA, ALASKA

I've felt this way three times in my life: the first time my dad blamed me for his drinking; the day my dad's credit card wouldn't go through at the vet's office; and now, with Tracer standing over me, knowing who I am. I can't hear anything but the thud of my own heart. My scalp feels like it's creeping backward toward my spine. This can't be happening. Not now.

"Lucy. Gotta admit I like it better than Barb. And so young, too." Tracer clucks his tongue like a mother hen.

"I don't know what you're talking about."

Tracer scratches his head. "Really? I could've sworn you turned around when I called you. Lucy, right? Lucy 'the Giant' Otsego?"

My throat feels like it's sealed shut. "Barb," I manage to say. "My name is Barbara."

"Barbara? Oh, well, maybe you're Lucy's sister?" I blink and my ears fill with the sound of seagulls, the engine, the wind. Suddenly I'm angry. Angry that I could lose everything in a split second. I'm not going to let it happen again. I'm not a child anymore. I'm an adult. I'm a giant. Lucy the Giant.

"Maybe I don't have time for this," I say, and walk away. Choke on it, Tracer.

It must work, because Tracer doesn't follow me and I have a minute to think.

C'mon, Lucy girl. You were expecting this. The minute you saw Dan with Tracer, you expected the worst. Of course I did. I usually get the worst. But not this time. I put my head in my hands. It's below zero out here today, but I feel hot. Tracer makes a shuffling sound from his perch, and I wonder what he's up to. I try to relax, look casual. I search the waves for the orcas again.

I have money on me, half my earnings so far. But there are no planes to hop in the middle of the sea. And I don't want to go. I promised Killit I'd come home.

What does Tracer want?

I hear another shuffling sound and realize that he's finally climbed down from the rigging. Maybe my bluff really did work, I think. Maybe he's given up already. But then the door to the wheelhouse slams and I go cold. He's turning me in to Harley.

A hot tear runs down my cheek. I slap it away. I can't seem to peel myself away from the railing. My fingers clench around the brass so tightly they turn white. I wait for the wheelhouse door to swing open again, for Harley's boots to come stomping across the deck, for the ax to fall.

But it doesn't come. I stay there squeezing the life out of the railing for another thirty minutes, and nothing happens. The stars don't fall from the sky. The world doesn't stop turning. And more importantly, Harley doesn't come out.

I have no idea what this means. I have no idea what to do.

By now the cold's so bad I'm starting to shiver. Cautiously, I head back toward the wheelhouse. Harley is behind the wheel. I stop midstride, waiting. He's so intent on scanning the water for our pots he hardly notices me. And when he does, he just gives me one of those smiles and says, "Coffee's on. Doesn't pay to get too cold out here."

I keep my mouth shut and move past him to the galley, where Geneva is playing solitaire like it's a normal Sunday afternoon. "Hey," she says.

"Hey."

I'm in the Twilight Zone. The bomb has dropped, and nobody's noticed the fallout.

I almost want to laugh. My bluff worked. Tracer was just shooting in the dark.

I go down the hall to the bathroom, shaking my head.

Tracer comes out of the john ahead of me. He fills the hallway and fixes me with the friendliest look in the world. "Hey, Bar-bar-ah," he says. He enunciates each syllable, like it's a new word to him. And then he grins at me. If I was a dog, the hair on the back of my neck would be up now. I'd be growling, barking. Or running away.

Instead, I just stand there, filling my own side of the hallway. He's just a bully, Lucy. You can stare him down. I won the survival suit fair and square. I can win this fight too. I stand a little taller.

But Tracer doesn't wait to be stared down. He pushes past me, almost politely, and says, "Excuse me."

Every fiber in my body is shaking. But to look at Tracer, there's no clue *anything* has happened. Except that grin. He still has the shadow of it on his face when he heads up to the galley, whistling as he goes.

I lock myself in the bathroom and try to control

my shakes. Geneva knocks on the door. "Feeling all right, hon? Crab's on. We gotta suit up."

I stand there looking at myself in the mirror and wonder what to do next. "Be right there."

I splash some water on my face and open the door. Geneva's already back on deck. The engines gutter out and I hear the anchor chains sliding down as we come to a full stop. It's time to go to work again.

For the next twenty hours we work so hard, hauling and sorting, that I don't have time to think. And Tracer doesn't have time to cause trouble. It's not until the next day, when the pots are emptied and we're chugging to the next spot, that the game begins.

"You guys've done well," Harley tells us after the last trap has been stowed. "Hold's full, so we'll be heading back to the processing plant tonight. Then we'll do one more run before this window shuts. Steak for supper. I'm cooking."

"Well, hallelujah for that!" Geneva exclaims, and shuffles inside for a cup of coffee. I follow her quickly, afraid to be left alone on deck with Tracer.

But it turns out being alone isn't the thing to fear.

We've peeled off our wet work clothes and are cozying up to the stove, when Tracer looks at me and says, "Barb, you know, you don't look like a Barb."

I say nothing. Stay low and stay out of the way. But it's hard to do when you're stuck in a tiny kitchen in the middle of nowhere with three people studying your face.

Geneva gives me the once-over. "Ah, she looks like a Barb to me."

"Nah," Harley joins in from the stove, where he's peppering up four huge T-bones on a tin plate. "I think she looks like an Elizabeth. Lizzie. Tin Lizzie." Even I have to smile at that one. Maybe this is going nowhere, after all.

"Lizzie . . . that's close." Tracer squints his eyes dangerously. "Nope. She looks like a Lucy to me," Tracer says.

The room falls silent. Oh God, oh God. My heart pounds in my chest. Everyone looks at me a minute longer. I'm going to die. "Had . . . had a dog . . . named Lucy, once," I stammer. My ears are burning. They must know I'm lying.

But Geneva laughs. Harley shrugs and turns away. "I still say Tin Lizzie."

"I don't know," Geneva says. "Maybe Tracer's on to something. A lot of people look like their dogs. Which explains Tracer, if you ask me."

Tracer makes a sour face, but everyone else laughs. I join in, a little late, a little forced, just so I don't stand out, and the moment passes.

Tracer is all but silent until the steaks come. The rest of us eat and joke the way we always do, but every once in a while I catch Tracer looking at me with what can only be read as pure hate.

The next morning we arrive at the processing barge bright and early. Harley comes back from haggling with a satisfied look on his face. "Twice the price I thought we'd get. Quite a chunk for four people. Might pay off the bills sooner and have something left over now too."

"Good for you, Harley." Geneva gives him a hug. "As for me, it's got to be a trip someplace warm, like Tahiti or Florida."

Tracer shrugs and swings up to his spot on the rigging. "I hear Sitka's nice this time of year, right, Barb?"

To my credit, I don't flinch. All the money in the world won't help me now. I wait for someone to take the bait—you've been to Sitka, Barb? That where you're from?

Instead, Geneva says, "To hell with Sitka—when I say warm, I mean out-of-Alaska warm. Heck, I could sit around *here* all summer if I wanted to stay in Alaska."

Thank God Geneva doesn't like Tracer. If she wasn't so busy looking to take a shot at him, she might get curious. As it is, I don't press my luck. "I'll go wash down the hold," I say to no one in particular, and sidle on out of there as fast as I can.

Tracer's not going to give up. It's like he's got my life held hostage, but so far, no ransom note. How do you strike a deal with a hijacker who doesn't want anything?

Fortunately, or not, a cat and mouse can't play forever. Eventually the mouse gets away. Or the cat gets hungry and stops playing. Less than an hour after Harley's announcement, Tracer finds me in the bunkroom alone.

"I want your share," he says. "All of it, from both fisheries, and I stay quiet."

"What? That's thousands of dollars, Tracer. Besides, there's nothing to stay quiet about." My bluff rings lamely in my ears this time, and he knows it too.

"Well, let's see." He holds out a hand and ticks off his fingers. "Underage, *and* a runaway. You could go to juvie-D for something like that. What is this—three months of hooky?"

"Nobody goes to jail for cutting school, Tracer." I start to push past him. He puts a hand out.

"Wait, wait, wait. I wonder what Fish and Game would think about a minor being on a crabbing boat. Dangerous work. Illegal, I think. It'd probably cost Harley his license. Maybe even his boat."

It's like hitting a brick wall at ninety miles an hour. If Harley loses the boat, he loses everything. Including his little girl.

"You wouldn't dare." I sound dangerous. Right now I am dangerous. I turn all my height, my weight, my *giantness* toward Tracer. Suddenly he seems so small, so easy to break, anything but an obstacle. I raise my hand and ball it into a fist.

Tracer goes pale. But only for a second. He's almost as tall as I am, and has probably gotten into more fights too.

"What you gonna do with that, little girl? Suck your thumb?"

"Go to hell."

He laughs. I feel ridiculous. Even worse, I feel small. Only my dad has ever been able to do that to me. If I give Tracer everything, I'll have nothing. No way to afford staying in Kodiak for the rest of the year. No way to avoid going back to my dad.

But hurting Harley isn't worth it. If I leave after this run, he won't find out about me. He won't hate me. And he'll still have his boat, his license. He'll still have both Miranda Lees.

"You win." My chest hurts. I feel weak, sick. I pull my little stash out of my backpack, toss it on his bunk, and walk away. More than anything, I want to reach the deck, to forget this ever happened.

"Oh, and Lucy?" I pause, afraid of what he'll say next. "I want Monroe's survival suit too."

It's not even worth turning around for. I keep going until I'm at the bow of the boat again, cutting through the icy waves, the water, blue and gray, washing all around me. I remember the dream I had that first week on the *Miranda Lee*. Bar was right. I had to wake up sometime.

Crabbing. Grab, yank, sort. Grab, yank, sort. There is no comfort in the rhythm anymore. Geneva stopped trying to joke with me yesterday. I know I should relax and enjoy the rest of the time I have on the *Miranda Lee*, but it's all gone sour now. It's like eating something you love until it makes you sick. You can never eat it again.

Somehow I feel more beaten down by Tracer than by anything my dad ever did to me. I guess back in Sitka I didn't have anything to lose until Bar. And when I did finally lose her, I didn't stick around to see how it would feel. I just left. Seems like there's got to be a time when staying low and out of the way isn't my only option. When I can just be me, giant or not, kid or grown-up.

But certainly not today. Tracer walks by me every once in a while, whistling or humming that old Beatles song, "Lucy in the Sky with Diamonds." I'm

starting to hate the song almost as much as I hate him.

I should've listened to my dreams. Maybe I wasn't ready for this. Maybe I should come clean to Harley. But it's too late for maybes. The damage is already done. My only hope is keeping Tracer quiet and happy. So I guess he wins.

"Last pot, guys, then we call it a season!" Harley shouts over the sounds of the engine. "Wind's picking up. We've got a storm coming our way." I haul double-time, with the help of the winch. When the pot comes up, Geneva and I both start yanking and sorting. Tracer ties down the other pots. He finishes his job before we finish ours and goes to join Harley in the wheelhouse.

If I'd been paying attention, I would've noticed it sooner. If I hadn't been so busy moping, I could have beaten him to the punch.

I walk into the wheelhouse to find Harley staring at me. He looks like he's been punched in the stomach. I stop so fast Geneva slams into me from behind.

"Whoops! Jeez, Barb . . ." She trails off, seeing Harley's face. And Tracer's sly smirk.

We all stand there, just staring at each other.

"Is it true?" Harley asks.

"I told you, the Coast Guard guy described her to a tee," Tracer says, that whine slipping back into his voice. Harley cuts him off with a hand in the air. He never stops looking at me.

"I know what Tracer said, but you tell me. Is it true? Is your name *Lucy* Otsego?"

I can't speak. I can't even blink, but I manage to nod.

He makes a sound like a whale letting air escape from its blowhole. Seconds tick by.

"Fifteen," he says, just above a whisper, and shakes his head.

Almost sixteen, I start to say. My birthday is in two months. But it doesn't matter. What matters is what everyone is thinking: Young. Too young.

That's the last time Harley looks at me. He leans on the wheel, looks at the floor, runs a hand through his hair. Does everything but look me in the eye. I close my eyes tight and open them again, but nothing changes.

For the first time since I've known her, Geneva stays quiet. Tracer, having gotten what he wants, chuckles. "I said *all* the money. Not half," he whispers as he passes me and walks away.

Half. I remember the envelope I left at Cap'n George's house and close my eyes. Tracer could have waited. He could have let me pay. But then I realize Tracer doesn't care about the money. Why would he, when it's more fun to hurt me?

"Ba—Lucy." Harley stumbles over my real name. "You're off the crew. Get downstairs. We're keeping you off deck until we get back. Then we'll deal with the authorities."

I don't move. I try to look him in the face. "I didn't mean to hurt anybody."

Harley turns back to the wheel. I glance at Geneva, but her face is completely closed to me. Tracer lurks in the doorway, looking smug. I try not to touch him as I squeeze by.

I feel more than see my way down the ladder to the hold. I'm numb. I can't feel anything.

With a rumble, the engines kick in. We start to move and I can hear the pounding of the waves signaling the approach of the next big storm.

CHAPTER 13

February 28

Bering Sea, Alaska

I've been down in the hold for longer than I can tell now. I don't know if it's because the *Miranda Lee* doesn't have a brig or if Harley and Geneva just don't want to have to look at me. I've tried sitting on the nets in the front of the hold, and I've tried pacing. Nothing works. With all the looks I used to get back home, bad as it felt, this is far worse. In Sitka I knew people looked at me because of my dad, or my size—things out of my control. But this I could have stopped. I should have stopped before I started. I just didn't think it through, right? After all, I'm just a kid.

Someone opens the door a crack and puts a dinner tray on the floor. I can't tell who it is. "Hello?" I call out. Whoever it is doesn't answer. They just walk away.

I don't think I've ever hurt anyone before. Not like

this. I'm usually so careful, so afraid of my own strength. No one told me I could crush somebody without ever touching them. I can't stop seeing the look on Harley's face when he sent me down here. I used to think I'd be glad if my dad even showed disappointment in me, so long as he bothered to take notice. Now that I've seen real disappointment, I'm not so sure.

The little tray has a slip of steak on it and some of Geneva's fried potatoes. I poke at the food and try to eat it because I want to show I'm grateful. But my stomach is in knots. So I sit there with my fork in my hand, sick, numb, and too hollow to cry. Eventually I fall asleep.

I'm having a nightmare. The room tilts sideways. I jolt awake. Far away I hear a voice scream, "Ice, we've got ice!" I can't clear my head, but I try. If I'm really awake, if we're in danger of sinking, I need to be out there on deck to help.

The door swings open easily when I shove it. They didn't lock me in, after all. I bite back a sob of fear, or maybe relief, and scrounge to find my deck gear. But it's been locked away in the wheelhouse. All I can find is Monroe's survival suit. Tracer hasn't claimed it for himself just yet.

I squeeze into the sleeves and seal myself in. I

climb the ladder, my chest on fire, afraid of what I'll find.

On deck it's worse than before. Worse than I ever thought it could be, because it's not a dream. The wind screams like a jet engine. Sleet cuts my cheeks. The *Miranda Lee* is listing deep into the water, on her side like a wounded whale. The pots are okay, covered in water-resistant tarps this time, so the ice water drains off before it has a chance to freeze. But the wheelhouse is a cube of frost. Every inch of railing, chain, and gear is boxed in like icing on a wicked cake.

"What the hell are *you* doing up here?" Tracer shouts at me.

"No kids on deck," Harley agrees. Even his shout above the storm sounds quiet to me. Disappointed. I almost forget the rain lashing at us, the ten-foot swipes the waves are launching over the deck.

Harley whales on the ice coating the wheelhouse, smashing it with all he's got. The others join in, Geneva looking small and fragile against the storm. With their backs to me they don't notice the wave. A wall of ice and water headed straight toward the aft deck where the lifeboat is secured. I move as fast as I can to check the lines. If the lifeboat goes, we're lost. But the wave doesn't take the lifeboat with its bright orange body, its room for ten. Instead, it takes me, picks me up in Monroe's survival suit like I was nothing, and tosses me overboard.

The water smashes against me so cold it feels like my heart's stopped beating. My face hurts. I scream, but the wind is louder. My damned survival suit can't do its job in this mess of wind, current, and pounding waves. I get churned under and start to sink. It's too late to even struggle—I can't tell which way is up.

I open my eyes wide, hoping for a clue, a tossed line, something. The ocean is bright as day. Tiny phytoplankton gleam around me, phosphorescent shrimplike bodies glowing pale green. The water crashes around my ears like breaking champagne glasses. I sink deeper into the sea.

They say your entire life flashes before you when you're drowning. I see Harley, the way he looked that first night at the Polar Bar. I see Tracer, hopping mad when I beat him at his own drinking game. Santa Barbara eating oatmeal in the driveway by the trash. My father cocking his arm back to slap me as I stumble to get Bar out of the house.

Water swallows me. It's beautiful down here. Cold, deep, softly quiet. A girl could get used to this. If she didn't have to breathe.

Ice and water fill my lungs. The pain shoots through me to my brain, and I see lights. I see stars. I see my mother's face.

And I realize, without a doubt, that this is all her fault.

You left me, Ma. You left me to drown in Sitka, in a pile of old bottles and change, under the weight of my dead-drunk dad. And not a word since then, not a card at Christmas, a birthday gift, nothing to let me know you were still around and you still cared.

If there's one thing you did give me, it was the ability to lie to the people I care about. You lied when you said you'd always love us. You lied when you said you'd always be there for me. And I'm lying now. I've lied to Harley, to Geneva, to Bar. I've even been lying to myself.

The cold sinks in and I realize I've been under longer than I thought. Ever since I was seven years old.

When my mother ran away, I wanted to run too. I wanted to leave Sitka and the pain of losing her behind me. But I wasn't like her. I didn't want to be like her. Someone who lets people down. And I had my father to look after. So I stayed.

Now look at me.

I've been running too.

Face it, Lucy. Disappearing into the sea now doesn't make much difference. You were erased a long time ago.

I see Harley and Geneva, Killit and Cap'n George. I

see Bar. I see Sheila. I see my dad on the sofa, waiting for my mother to walk back through that door. Waiting for me.

And I know I have to go back. You can't run forever, Lucy girl. If you do, eventually you have to leave everyone behind. Even the ones you love.

By sheer force of will I roll onto my back, hoping the survival suit will do its job and I'll float toward the surface. Nothing happens. I will die here. Like a whale at sea.

Something moves, swimming toward me. It gets closer, and I gasp even though I can't breathe. I am not dreaming. I am face to face with an orca.

The whale is beautiful, white tracing on a black body so massive that even I feel tiny beside it. It bounces me lightly with its nose. The heart-deep, singing clicks of its voice fill the water around us. I wonder if this is one of the pod I saw pass us by two days ago, drawn by the soft light of the plankton. Maybe it's here to rescue me.

I float, breathless, and remember my mom's story about how people and animals used to live together long ago. And how sometimes a whale could be a woman and marry a man, have a little girl. And then return to the sea. But what about the daughter? I never asked before. I guess the kid gets to choose for herself.

In a rush of water the whale swims away from me. It turns around and gently flicks me with its unimaginable flukes. Twisting in the water from the nudge, I watch the orca swim away only to be replaced by another shape rising to meet me. No, not rising. Falling. It falls from the surface and somehow I know I have been saved after all. The orca has turned me around. And what I see is not another whale, but a human being. Tracer.

His eyes are wild with fear, his hands clawing at a line twisted around him. He's drowning and fighting it with all his might. But his clothes are both too heavy and too thin. Without a survival suit he'll last only a few minutes.

I could just watch him die. Some kids would. Some adults, too. But not me.

I kick as hard as I can and launch myself toward him. He slams into my giant arms and I hold him, trying to get him to calm down.

Tracer screams underwater and the bubbles blind me. I realize we'll both drown if he doesn't stop fighting and let me help him. So I do the only thing I can. I hit him. I pull back my arm and swing at him, a slow-motion drag through the salty water. Still, it's strong enough. His head snaps back and he sags, no longer fighting. I should feel good. How many times have I wanted to punch him? But I'm too scared, too tired to feel anything more. I move him into a survival carry and slowly, painfully drag myself toward the surface, praying the *Miranda Lee* is there to save us both.

"Damn it, Barb! You scared me!" A hand hauls me, pulling at the collar of my survival suit in vain. Soon one of the pot hooks joins in and snags my leg.

"Take Tracer," I gasp. The words burn as I try to suck air back into my lungs. It's raining in the outside world now. The storm must've died down while Tracer and I were under.

Tracer is dragged from my arms, coughing water, and at last I am hauled aboard. For the first time I realize I'm freezing. Harley half-drags me into the cabin, ripping open the suit like he's gutting a fish, cursing all the while.

"Harley." I'm shaking and so cold that all my tears are frozen. I want to say I'm sorry, to say I couldn't go away, but all that comes out is his name.

"Shut up and stay warm. We've got you now." And I know Geneva is there too, working on Tracer.

"Damn, he's cold," she says, stripping down and climbing into the bunk with him in her long johns. Body heat is still the best way to keep warm.

"Harley," I whisper again, but he doesn't hear me, because he's taking off his parka. I'm too big for

Geneva to warm up. Harley has to stay with me. He climbs onto my cot, wraps me in a big blanket, and puts his arms around me in a hug I haven't felt since I was tiny. A hug I haven't felt since I was a little girl.

"Sorry, Daddy," I whisper, and fall into a cold, watery sleep.

CHAPTER 14

February 29

KODIAK, ALASKA

Tracer and I are out of danger. He sits wide awake in the bunk across from mine, his hands wrapped in gauze and propped up on pillows. He might lose two of his fingers to frostbite and one to the line that wrapped around him when he went overboard. I'm lucky. The survival suit actually did its job and kept me alive.

Tracer doesn't make a sound. Neither do I. I don't know what to say.

Geneva comes in with a bowl of soup for me, a cup of hot sugar water for Tracer. The sugar is supposed to help with the frostbite somehow. Geneva looks more tired than I've ever seen her. "How're we doing?"

She pulls a chair up to Tracer's bunk and helps him take a sip from the cup. He makes a face.

"This stuff makes my teeth hurt."

Geneva pulls back. "Must be feeling better if you're complaining, huh?"

I have yet to hear either Geneva or Harley complain, though. Geneva's hands are raw from hauling the line that pulled us in. And Harley, she tells me, broke a rib hauling my water-filled survival suit to safety. The *Miranda Lee* is lucky to be limping home. We'll be in Kodiak by nightfall.

"How about you?" Geneva drags her chair over to my bed. "You ready to talk to us now?" I haven't spoken a word to anyone since I was rescued.

I sit up in my bunk to cradle the bowl of soup she offers me. "Thank you for the soup."

Geneva laughs. "That's all you've got to say?"

"No."

I look away for a second at the gray waves under the rainy sky. I want to say I'm sorry. I want to say how much I love being here. But mostly I just want to tell the truth. About everything.

"My name is . . ." I hesitate. From his bunk, Tracer is listening. But I guess he has a right to hear this too.

"My dog's name was Santa Barbara. Mine is Lucy. Lucy the Giant."

I laugh. For the first time the nickname doesn't sound so bad. After months of being Barbara, Lucy the Giant sounds more like who I really am.

Geneva listens patiently. Even Tracer is quiet for the moment.

"Santa Barbara was all I had. When she died, I couldn't go home again. I ended up at the airport, mixed in with a work charter. And that got me here."

"To the Polar Bar," Geneva adds. She sucks in a breath. "Jesus, hon, why didn't you tell us? We could have helped you."

I look her in the eye. "How?"

Geneva studies her hands. "I don't know. But we would have tried."

A tear spills over my lower eyelid and runs in a hot track down my cheek. I shrug it off. I couldn't bear the pity look from Geneva.

"Well, I've been doing a lot of thinking." I put the soup bowl down on the bed. It sloshes but doesn't spill. "And I think maybe . . ."

Geneva sits back in her seat. "Yeah?"

"I'm going back home."

"Not so fast." Harley stands in the doorway. "I have a pretty good idea of what you left behind in Sitka. There's no reason you can't stay here." He gives Tracer a hard look. Tracer looks away. His eyes go to his hands, resting on their pillows. He nods almost imperceptibly. He won't give me away.

Harley clears his throat. "Barbara Otsego is a respected member of the Kodiak community, and a necessary part of this crew. It can stay that way." He comes into the room, stands by Geneva's chair.

"Does anyone here object?"

Geneva raises her eyebrows. Tracer coughs but doesn't say anything.

"I do." All eyes turn toward me.

I put the soup bowl on the floor and climb out of bed. My legs feel weak, but I stand anyway.

"Lucy—" Harley starts to protest.

"Harley, I can't be Barbara forever. It's not right." My legs start to buckle and I sit down on the bed.

"If there's one thing I'm learning about being an adult, it's that you have to be responsible. At least for yourself." I look at their faces—Geneva nods slowly. Harley rubs his eyes.

"I learned that from you, Harley."

Geneva gets up and waves her hand in the air. "Well, Skipper, you've created a monster." She smiles at me. "You sure you're only fifteen?"

"Yes." I smile back.

"Well, Harley, you talk some sense into her, if you can. But that sounds about right to me. Honey, I'll help you any way I can. But for now I guess I'll leave you two alone." She heads for the door.

"What about me?" Tracer asks. For the first time it isn't a whine.

Geneva pauses in the doorway. "Can you walk?"

"I don't think so."

"Well." She turns back around. "I guess I'll stay here. Harley, you and Lucy scoot."

"Yes, ma'am." Harley holds out his hand. He helps me up from the bed. Together we hobble into the galley.

I drop down into a seat at the galley table.

Harley looks at me and shakes his head. "Last night when I pulled you from the water, do you know what you said to me?"

I shake my head. "I probably said I was sorry. I meant it."

"No." He gives me a bemused look. "You called me Daddy." He pauses, shakes his head again. "Lucy, nobody's said that to me in almost seven years."

My face flushes red with embarrassment. When I speak, I stammer, but I tell the truth. "I—I must've meant it, huh?"

Harley doesn't laugh at me. And he doesn't tell me to go away. Instead, he comes over and pulls me into a hug.

"Take care, Lucy. Everything's going to be all right."

For the first time in months, I get to be fifteen again. I hug him back hard enough to last a lifetime.

Tracer was right after all. Kids who run away do go to jail. The day after we dock in Kodiak, Harley, Geneva, and the captain see me off at the airport. But instead of flying straight to Sitka, I go to the state capital, Juneau. A woman is waiting for me.

"Hi, Lucy." She blinks and stands a little straighter. Until now she must have doubted my size. "Your friend Geneva called ahead."

"She said that the state has programs for people like my dad. That you might be able to help."

"I certainly hope so. I'm Mrs. Saunders. I'm your court-assigned social worker. You'll stay with us at Johnson Youth Center until the hearing tomorrow."

"My dad actually said he would come?"

"Yes, he did. That's a good sign, Lucy. We all want things to be better for you both."

The youth center isn't as bad as you might think. I sit in my room on a cot not much fancier than the bunks on the *Miranda Lee,* and try to imagine why my dad would be willing to come and get me.

My father comes to the hearing sober. He's cleaned himself up a bit—a shave, his hair combed back. He's even found a shirt with no stains and an old sports coat to wear. I marvel at the effort. Why fight to keep something you never wanted in the first place? But then I guess there are other things at stake here. Maybe he's facing jail time for neglect. Maybe he's facing rehabilitation.

It's not a hearing really, not with a courtroom and a bunch of people sitting in the jury box. Instead, it's held in an office with three chairs on one side of a big desk and a high-backed leather chair on the other. The judge sits in the leather chair, in a gray suit, not the black robes you see on TV. He looks like a teacher or a doctor to me.

"Mr. Otsego, we're here today to determine the best living situation for you and your daughter." The judge smiles at me. "Now, Lucy, I understand you lived with your father up until recently. Can you tell me why you left?"

I blink. How can I tell him? How can I tell him that years of being the wrong size for your life, the wrong kid for your dad, the wrong everything, builds up until you can't take it anymore? I can't. Instead, I give the simplest reason. The one I gave everyone on the *Miranda Lee*.

"My dog died."

The judge clears his throat. My dad says nothing. I doubt he even remembers I had a dog.

"I'm sorry," the judge finally says. I think he actually means it. "So are you telling me your father had nothing to do with your running away?"

"He could have helped me save her. He didn't."

The judge looks down, and I can't tell if he's avoiding eye contact or reading the papers on the desk in front of him.

He turns to my dad, but my dad is looking at me. I flush under his stare and think of what I said to Harley. *Sorry, Daddy*. Sorry, Dad, that we couldn't be much of a family. But now it's up to you and me. The judge leans forward and puts his elbows on his desk.

"Mr. Otsego, I understand you've had some difficulties in the past with drinking?"

"Yes, sir," my father says. He admits it. The sky doesn't fall, the world doesn't turn backward. But nothing changes, either.

"You've gone through our rehabilitation program?"

My father clears his throat. "Yes." My father's been the way he is for over seven years. I never saw him try to change. I turn to see his expression, to see if what he says is true. But his face is unreadable.

"How long ago?" the judge asks.

My dad shifts in his seat. "A couple years."

"Then you know family record counts when it comes to financial assistance?"

"Yes."

I close my eyes. I see his angle after all. My dad is here for money. Not for me.

The judge scans his papers. "Are you currently employed?"

"Not at this time. No." My dad coughs into his hand.

"Well, Mr. Otsego. It looks like your temporary assistance is almost up. I suggest you find yourself a job in the next two months, or you may very well end up back in my office."

My dad nods. "Yessir." I hang my head. Two months on the Bering Sea pays more money than my dad gets in half a year. Imagine that, cashed out in empty bottles on the floor.

The judge looks straight at my father for a minute, and my dad looks back. "Mr. Otsego, give me one reason why Lucy should live with you."

I open my eyes. I need to hear this too.

My dad rubs his jaw with rough fingers but holds the judge's stare. When he speaks, his voice sounds hollow. Like he's given this speech before.

"This girl's mother left when she was just a kid, Your Honor. Such as I am, I'm all she's got."

I swallow hard. Whether he means it or not, I know it's not true. I've never had my dad, not since I can remember, not like a real family. But I have Harley, Geneva, Cap'n George, Don—everyone in Kodiak. If only that counted for something here, in this room.

I look at the judge and at my dad. My fate is stuck somewhere between them. No, Lucy, I remind myself. What happens from now on is up to you.

The judge closes his file. "Well, Miss Otsego, I don't see that there is a better alternative for you at this point. Your school records indicate you're smart and capable. And you have no other relatives that I can see. Go home with your father, Lucy, and see if you can make it work. Sometimes family is the best thing."

My father doesn't say a single word to me on the trip home. The pickup truck has a few extra dents in it from his most recent late-night binges. We drive onto the ferry at the Juneau docks and wait out the nine-hour ride home to Sitka.

We arrive at six o'clock in the morning. I've been awake most of the night. Used to different hours, I guess.

Mount Edgecumbe is not as beautiful as I remember, or as big. Something inside me melts like ice against front teeth, cold, painful, and slow. Sitka and I have both changed.

The house still looks like a kid that lost a fight, and Dad's boat project is just as sorry as ever. But now the yard looks smaller, more run-down. I never thought of our house as beautiful, but back then it was all I knew.

I climb the stairs to my tiny bedroom in the attic, toss my duffel on the floor, and hit my elbows on the walls trying to take off my coat. It's suffocating in here. I drop to the little bed and open the window, sticking my head out for fresh air.

The next day is a school day. The yard is crowded with tons of kids screaming and screeching like seagulls. I miss the quiet hum of the *Miranda Lee*. I didn't fit in at school when I left it, and that, at least, hasn't changed. I can't remember where my locker is, so I don't try to find it. Instead, I walk across Mrs. Krupke's classroom and take a seat by the window, where I can watch the water.

I'm going to make it through two more years of being Lucy the Giant. I just don't know how.

"Psst." A note skids across my desk. I glance up to see Sheila give a little wave. She looks scared to see me. My fingers feel too thick to open the little piece of paper easily. I fumble for a few seconds, then finally get it undone.

It's a skinny stick-figure drawing of Sheila holding out a flower. *Sorry. I told you my brother was a jerk. Are you okay?*

No one—not Mrs. Saunders, not my dad, not even the judge asked me that. Am I okay? I have to think about it for a while. Finally I draw a giant crab—a pretty realistic one, I must admit—accepting the flower. *Yeah. A little crabby, maybe. But I'll survive.*

I toss the note back to Sheila and she smiles. When class is over, she's waiting right outside the door.

"Oh. My. God. When you didn't show up for class the first week, I thought something terrible had happened. I tried to go by your house, but no one was home."

"My dad probably was. He just doesn't answer the door."

"Jesus, Lucy. What was it like? I'd give anything to run away some days, just to get away from all of this. . . ." She waves her hands around at the normalcy, at the kids just like her, doing exactly what they should be doing.

Suddenly I need to get some air. I push through the crowds toward the door.

Sheila follows and plops down on the steps beside me.

"Sorry. I really am, Luce. I knew things weren't great for you, but I didn't know they were that bad, either. I don't deserve to be your friend."

"Friend?" I taste the word. "We're friends."

Sheila smiles, and for a second I can see Geneva in her. "Yeah," I say. "I guess we are."

Sheila swats me on the arm. "Of course we're

friends. Why do you think I was so miserable without you?"

Before I know it, tears fill my eyes. "I . . . didn't know you were. All I could think about was getting away. I never stopped to think I was leaving anything . . . or anyone behind."

Sheila throws her skinny little arm around my shoulder and gives me a great big hug. "Lucy, I think maybe everybody is lonely. And we just don't know enough to talk about it."

I picture Harley sitting there on the *Miranda Lee* all alone, missing his little girl. "Yeah. I think you might be right."

I come straight home after school, part of my agreement with the judge. No more loitering, pretending not to be a minor. Truancy, he told me, will be punishable by law.

The pickup truck is still in the front yard, which means my dad is home. I dump my bag in the mudroom and go into the kitchen. The usual pile of booze money is sitting there, but the house is quiet. I stare at the bills littering the table, then start to count them. "We really should be putting all this cash in the bank," I say to no one in particular. The house stays silent. I look around. There's a pile of mail by the door. This time I'm glad my dad didn't throw it out. A brown box from the Sitka Animal Hospital sits beneath the junk mail and late bills. Bar's ashes. It's like she's come back to me.

I drop to the floor and pull the box into my lap. Ripping the tape with my house key, I reach inside. I pull out a tin can, too big for soup, too small for paint, wrapped in plain green paper.

I press my cheek to the rough wrapping. Santa Barbara.

I sit there for a few minutes, trying to remember her face, her sandy brown fur, her serious eyes. So much has happened since the day she died. I feel like I've died too, and come back to life again. And all that time, I barely gave myself a chance to miss her.

But I miss her now.

Staring over the edge of her can, over the top of her box, I feel like crying, but the tears won't come. After what seems like a long time, I pick up the can and start to stand. A second package catches my eye. The envelope is thick and addressed to me. Postmarked Kodiak.

I take a quick breath and sit down at the table to rip it open. Inside is a letter from Cap'n George wrapped around another envelope—my envelope. It still smells like turkey and cranberry sauce. I unfold the letter and start to read.

Dear Lucy,

(That'll still take some getting used to, I think. You sure did look like a Barbara to me.) You can imagine my surprise last night when I went for a midnight snack and came up with an envelope full of cash. A remnant of your ill-gotten gains, I suspect. Well, every girl should have a college fund. Now, put it in a proper bank and you're on your way. It was a pleasure having you. Visit when you have the chance.

Affectionately,
Cap'n George (and Killit)

"You would have liked Killit," I whisper, touching Bar's can. And then I laugh, because it seems ridiculous that my family should be reduced to this—a can of ashes and an envelope full of cash. The laugh turns to tears, tears for Bar, for Harley and the captain, for Geneva and life on the *Miranda Lee*. For every good thing I've had in my life.

And then, eventually, the tears stop for all the same reasons. Bar, Kodiak, they're from another lifetime. But it was my lifetime. Before I met Bar, I would have said it was all impossible. Now I know everything is possible. Even for me.

I open the other envelope. All the money is there. Every single dollar. I look at the little pile of money on the table. Drinking money. My dad's money. It's true, kids don't have many choices. Lucy the Giant didn't. But Barb the Adult did. I leave my dad's cash on the table and head out to put *my* money where it can give Lucy, the future adult, all the options she'll ever need.

"Lucy?"

My heart skips a beat. My dad has been sitting in the living room on the sofa the whole time.

I hold my tongue.

"Luce. I know you're there."

"Yessir." I drag myself to the doorway to see what he wants.

He's still in his court clothes a day later. But then I move a little closer and see that these are actually different clothes. Dressed up two days in a row. It's a miracle.

"Job interview," he explains.

For a moment I actually dare to hope. Maybe the world is spinning in a different direction. Maybe my dad can change. But then he rinses his mouth with a beer. Whatever promise the words held disappear.

"Some damn plant job."

"Whatever." Some things never change. I turn to leave when he calls out again.

"How was it?"

"How was what?"

"The, y'know . . ." He's already starting to slur. I just want to get out of here. I want my money in a bank account where it can grow and turn into wings that can fly me back to Kodiak, to the captain and Killit, to Geneva and, most of all, to Harley. But my dad, my real dad, is asking me a question. I hang my head and say again, "How . . . was . . . what?"

"The crabbin', girl. The catch."

I can't believe it. I turn around again to face my dad. He's sitting there with a light in his eyes. A light I've never seen there before. Fevered, maybe, blurred by beer and years of damage, but it's there. And I recognize it. It's the same fire I felt whenever the *Miranda Lee* set sail. And then I remember. Long ago, before he became my dad the failure, he was my dad the fisherman.

Like father, like daughter after all.

"It was good, Dad. Really good."

He chuckles to himself and snorts, spluttering some of his beer. I go get a towel to clean up his mess. But then I stop.

Tonight I will get a call from Murph's bar telling me to bring my daddy home. And tomorrow at McDonald's, Vickie Drake will smile her tight little smile and feel sorry for me again. Welcome home, Lucy, she'll say. Welcome home.

I drop the towel on the kitchen counter. It's time

to stop, Lucy girl. For the first time I realize there is a difference between running and walking away.

I pick my bag up off the floor and leave my dad to his messes. And this time, when I go out, it's not through the mudroom, but through the front door.

EPILOGUE

June 4

SITKA, ALASKA

I finally finished reading *The Old Man and the Sea.* I felt a bit guilty dropping it back in the box when Mrs. Krupke asked us to return our books. My copy had suffered through unimaginable trials while I was on the *Miranda Lee*. It makes me wonder if all those ripped-up copies have been to the Bering Sea.

School is over for the year, and the salmon are running just north of here. In her last letter Geneva told me the *Miranda Lee* will be heading out next week for her share. Tracer was true to his word. He's left crabbing and moved on to the processing plants. The accident and his injuries soured him to real offshore work. As far as everyone in Kodiak knows, I was just another seasonal crabber who left in the spring.

So Harley gets to keep his license and his boat. At the end of the summer he's even going to see his little

girl. Don's taking the season off, so they've hired three new crewmen on the *Miranda Lee*. They're not like the old crew. How could they be?

Today is so beautiful it seems a shame to stay inside. Bar's can has been collecting dust on the windowsill of my little room all spring long. I think I'll give her a proper burial today at the edge of the totem park where she used to follow me. She'll have a nice view of the harbor from there.

The sun is shining through big puffy clouds as I head outside. Even though spring is just about over, there are still whales passing through the channel. I can hear them as I head down the hill and enter the park's tall stand of pines.

The totem poles rise out of the mist like pillars in a giant cathedral. It's quiet here. Soft and deep with pine needles. Peaceful. I pass a couple of joggers, a family headed toward the picnic grounds, and make my way to a little patch of grass above the rocky beach.

"Well, girl, how's this?" I find a good place with a view beneath one of the pine trees. "Straight out to sea. You can even see Edgecumbe from here. Nice, huh?"

The ground is soft. I dig a little hole with my hands and bury the can in the earth.

"I love you, Bar. I promise to visit as much as I can." I sit with her for a while, watching the waves, listening to people laughing across the water, smelling the sea. It's beautiful. And, for the moment at least, I fit in, right where I belong.

About the Author

Sherri L. Smith has worked in animation, film, comic books, and construction. Her limited crabbing career started and ended with a garbage can and a string on the shores of the Chesapeake Bay. Currently she lives in Los Angeles, more than three thousand miles from the Bering Sea. This is her first young adult novel.